FINDING THE COWBOY'S FAMILY

ROWDY RANCH

Vicki Lewis Thompson

Ocean Dance Press

FINDING THE COWBOY'S FAMILY
© 2024 Vicki Lewis Thompson

ISBN: 978-1-63803-919-8

Ocean Dance Press LLC
PO Box 69901
Oro Valley, AZ 85737

This is a work of fiction. Any resemblance to actual persons, living or dead, business establishments, events, or locales is entirely coincidental.

Visit the author's website at
VickiLewisThompson.com

"**I've struggled with not feeling good enough.** My father's a plonker and my mum ran off and left me. But Granny and Grandpa treated me like I was pure gold. Granny still does. That's helped."

"You are pure gold."

That brought Kieran to a dead stop. "What?"

"A poet named Maya Angelou said *When someone shows you who they are, believe them the first time.*"

"I think I've heard that, but—"

"You've shown me who you are. You're brave, strong and persistent. You care about others. You're the real deal, Kieran. I'm just sad we won't… that we can't…."

"Me, too." Shoving aside all the voices in his head telling him it was a mistake, he reached for Sara.

She didn't resist when he pulled her close, but she didn't nestle against him either. Instead of winding her arms around his neck, she laid her palms against his chest. "We shouldn't."

"I know." Taking off his hat, he dipped his head under the brim of hers. "But I'm not as strong as you think."

Want more cowboys? Check out these other titles by
Vicki Lewis Thompson

Rowdy Ranch
Having the Cowboy's Baby
Stoking the Cowboy's Fire
Testing the Cowboy's Resolve
Rocking the Cowboy's Christmas
Roping the Cowboy's Heart
Tempting the Cowboy's Sister
Craving the Cowboy's Kiss
Heating Up the Cowboy's Christmas
Wrangling the Cowboy's Dreams
Blowing the Cowboy's Mind
Finding the Cowboy's Family

The Buckskin Brotherhood
Sweet-Talking Cowboy
Big-Hearted Cowboy
Baby-Daddy Cowboy
True-Blue Cowboy
Strong-Willed Cowboy
Secret-Santa Cowboy
Stand-Up Cowboy
Single-Dad Cowboy
Marriage-Minded Cowboy
Gift-Giving Cowboy

The McGavin Brothers
A Cowboy's Strength
A Cowboy's Honor
A Cowboy's Return
A Cowboy's Heart
A Cowboy's Courage

A Cowboy's Christmas
A Cowboy's Kiss
A Cowboy's Luck
A Cowboy's Charm
A Cowboy's Challenge
A Cowboy's Baby
A Cowboy's Holiday
A Cowboy's Choice
A Cowboy's Worth
A Cowboy's Destiny
A Cowboy's Secret
A Cowboy's Homecoming

Sons of Chance
What a Cowboy Wants
A Cowboy's Temptation
Claimed by the Cowboy
Should've Been a Cowboy
Cowboy Up
Cowboys Like Us
It's Christmas, Cowboy
Count on a Cowboy
The Way to a Cowboy's Heart
Trust in a Cowboy
Only a Cowboy Will Do
Wild About the Cowboy
Cowboys and Angels
A Last Chance Christmas

1

Kieran Haggerty eased his rented vehicle into a diagonal parking space in front of a shop called Hannigan's Western Wear. No doubt his granny would say finding an Irish establishment in the middle of Wagon Train was a sign.

He switched off the engine with a sigh of relief. Driving on the wrong side of the road all the way from the Missoula airport had been a challenge, especially with the massive lorries blocking his view.

But it could've been far worse. His mates had advised him to avoid jet lag by staying a night in New York. That had allowed him to book a morning flight out and make this drive in the middle of the day.

And a grand day it was. The August sun warmed his shoulders and the back of his neck when he climbed out of the vehicle.

He'd chosen to come in summer since he didn't fancy battling snow and ice on this trip. His granny was worried enough about him as it was. After all, her only daughter had never returned from her journey to America thirty years ago.

To calm his granny's fears, he'd bought her a mobile and taught her how to text so they could keep in touch. Speaking of that, he'd send her a picture of Hannigan's Western Wear. She'd still be awake if she'd been playing cards with the neighbors.

He stepped up on the curb and zeroed in on the name lettered over the door. Then he added a message. *I'm in Wagon Train. And look! A sign! Literally.* He tacked on a laughing face emoji.

His granny wasn't a fan of technology but she loved emojis. She chose images that caught her eye. Sometimes they fit the occasion, sometimes not. And if her finger slipped, anything was possible. She'd let it stand rather than trust the delete key.

Tucking away his mobile, he took note of his surroundings. The dog-eared postcard in his shirt pocket showcased the village from a different angle, but he still recognized the stone facade of the bank and the carved wooden doorway of the hotel next door.

The row of black lamp posts on either side of the street looked freshly painted and the footpath was free of litter. He appreciated that kind of civic pride.

Gazing toward the end of the street, he located the Fluffy Buffalo. The pub had come up during his online search to see if he could get a pint of Guinness in Wagon Train. He could and he would. After he'd bought a Stetson.

He'd spent years saving for this trip, fully aware the trail would grow fainter with time. By now it might have disappeared. Maybe he'd find no trace of his mum, but he wouldn't go home empty-handed. He'd leave town wearing a Stetson purchased at Hannigan's.

As he took a step toward the entrance, his mobile pinged. Pausing, he took it out of his pocket.

You made it, then. Hannigan's it is. Do they have kin over here?" A four-leaf clover was followed by a dartboard and a weightlifter.

I'll ask.

Did you get the hat you've gone on about? She added a hat-wearing face along with a palm tree and an elephant.

He texted back. *Soon. I'll take a picture.*

What's the time there?

Almost two.

Did you eat? She sent the licking lips face.

After I get the hat.

Promise? The weightlifter showed up again along with a rabbit.

Promise.

Bye, bye, then. This is costing you. A couple of hearts were followed by a whole row of flamingos.

Sending her a hug and a kiss, he disconnected. It was costing him, and she worried about that, too. But he'd created a budget that included an international calling plan, knowing she felt the distance between them like a knife in her heart. At this very moment she'd be lighting a candle and offering up a prayer to St. Joseph for his safekeeping.

Putting away his mobile, he crossed to the shop door and grasped the polished brass knob.

Like many things in this village, the doorknob had a timelessness that appealed to him.

He stepped inside and was immediately dazzled. The earthy tang of leather blended with the crisp aroma of denim. Western hats of many different shades covered an entire wall, and boots of all colors lined the shelves of the opposite wall.

Racks of yoked shirts in every pattern and color imaginable took up space in the center of the shop, along with jeans and jackets in a mixture of plain and highly decorated styles. He was in cowboy country. Completely out of his element.

A young lad and his father were trying on boots, and two women — one ginger-haired and the other a brunette — stood over by the hat wall. The ginger had sparkles on the back pockets of her jeans but her sleeveless white top had no decorations at all. She secured her handbag over her shoulder, picked up a navy hat and settled it on her head. Then she stepped in front of a full-length mirror.

The other woman, who looked to be seven or eight months along judging from the round belly under her loose-fitting top, made enthusiastic comments about how grand the hat looked. Since she had no handbag, he made a guess she was a salesperson.

He wandered in that direction. The navy hat was a good choice. It complemented the bright waves that cascaded to the woman's shoulders. As he approached, he caught her reflection in the mirror. His breath stalled. Green eyes, full lips, rosy cheeks. *Beautiful.* And familiar. As if he'd met her somewhere, which was impossible.

Her startled gaze locked with his and she turned. "Well, hello there. Where'd you come from?" Interest filled her expression. And a hint of delight.

His tongue stuck to the roof of his mouth. Eventually he got it to work again. "County Kildare." She wouldn't have heard of his tiny village so might as well not mention it.

"You're from Ireland?"

"That I am." And she wasn't from Montana. She didn't sound like the folks who'd rented him the vehicle in Missoula. Instead her accent put him in mind of the woman at the hotel desk in New York. "Do you live in Wagon Train?"

"No, not me. My two brothers do, though, and they never once mentioned an Irishman. How long have you lived here?"

"I'm visiting. Been in town all of fifteen minutes. I'm looking for a hat."

"You've come to the right place." The other woman smiled and held out her hand. "Welcome to Wagon Train and welcome to our store. I'm Justine Neubauer."

"Not Hannigan?"

"I'm Justine Hannigan Neubauer. My mom and dad took over from my grandparents and now my husband Eddie and I run the place. Mostly. My folks still pitch in now and then."

"And I'm Sara Armstrong." The beauty with the green eyes reached out her hand.

"Kieran Haggerty." He enjoyed her firm grip and held on a little longer than was polite, but she didn't seem to mind. "Where're you from, Sara?"

"New Jersey." She grinned. "I don't sound any more like the locals than you do. Are you with a tour?"

He shook his head. "I'm not. And before I forget—" Which he would if he kept staring at her. Releasing her hand, he turned to Justine. "My granny wants to know if any of the Hannigans came over from Ireland."

"I think so, way back. I have an aunt in Indiana who's into genealogy. She could give you the whole scoop. How long will you be staying?"

"A week."

"Then I'll have time to contact her and let you know. Did your granny come with you?"

"No, she's not a traveler. And that's a massive understatement. She and my grandpa went to Limerick on their honeymoon. Longest trip she's ever taken."

"You flew over by yourself?" Sara's forehead puckered.

He smiled. "I wouldn't say that. Every flight was jammers."

"That's not what I meant."

"Just joking. Yes, I'm on my own."

Justine looked confused, too. "Is Hannigan's why you settled on coming to Wagon Train?"

That made him laugh. "Not at all. I'd never heard of your shop. It was a surprise to discover an establishment with an Irish name so I texted Granny a picture and she wanted me to ask."

Sara continued to study him, a slight crease between her eyebrows. "Although it's none of my business, I'm dying to know. Why Wagon Train?"

Before he could answer, she lit up.

"Oh! I'll bet it's M.R. Morrison!"

"Who?"

"The author. The announcement just came out about her."

"Did she die?"

"No, she...." Smiling, she gave a little shrug. "It's not important. I'm being nosy."

"I don't mind saying why I'm here." Sara wouldn't be a source of information, but Justine's parents would have been running the shop at the time the postcard was mailed.

He pulled it out of his shirt pocket. "Thirty years ago my mum traveled to America with a man named Ronny Smith, a plonker, for sure. She sent postcards along the way, and this is the last one that came. We never heard from her again."

Sara's breath hitched. "Thirty years ago?"

"That's a long time," Justine said, her voice soft.

"I doubt she's alive. A postcard isn't much to go on, but if there's any chance I can find out what happened to her...."

"Of course." Compassion darkened Sara's green eyes. "How old were you when she left?"

"Barely two. Granny convinced her not to take me."

She nodded. "Good for your granny."

"I'll find out what my folks know," Justine said. "Do you have a picture?"

"I do, yeah." Plucking his wallet from his back pocket, he took out the worn photo of him sitting on her lap. Her long dark hair was wavy like his. Although the picture didn't show her eye color well, Granny said she'd had green eyes. Did he remember? Almost.

"Let me get my phone." Justine hurried over to the sales counter.

"I'll take a picture of it, too." Sara pulled a mobile out of her handbag and glanced at him. "If that's okay."

"It's better than letting the original out of my sight."

"You should never do that." She leaned in to get the shot, bringing her intriguingly spicy scent closer. "She's very pretty."

How kind of her to use the present tense.

"I suppose that's you."

"Yes."

"You were a cute baby."

"Most are at that age."

Justine returned with her mobile and quickly took a picture of the photo. "I'll show it to Mom and Dad first chance I get and see if they remember. Did you say her name? I didn't catch it if you did."

"Freya." He turned the postcard over so her signature was visible, in case Justine didn't know how to spell it.

His mum had made a production of signing her name — an elaborate F, a big loop for the y and a flourish at the end. "Freya Haggerty."

"Got it." She made a note on her mobile and took down his number. "If they had any contact with her at all, I think they'll remember a woman from Ireland visiting Wagon Train."

"I hope so."

"I'll let you know." She glanced up. "Can you guys hang here for a bit while I help those two with their boot purchase? Eddie's at the barber's so it's just me for the next thirty minutes or so."

He nodded. "I can wait."

"We'll be fine, Justine. I'll see if I can sell him a hat."

"Go for it."

As she hurried away, Sara turned to him. "Obviously I don't know anything about your mom since I don't even live here, but I'm staying with people who might have information."

"Oh?"

"It so happens I'm visiting for a week, too. If you're open to it, I'd like to help."

What an amazing offer. "But you're on holiday. You must have plans."

"Sure, but they're flexible. Nothing's a command performance except the combined birthday celebration for my sister and brother on Saturday night."

His heartbeat quickened at the prospect of spending more time with her. He was strongly attracted, but he could dial it back. This wasn't the time or the place. Besides, anyone who looked like her would surely have someone special in New Jersey.

He met her gaze. "Then thank you. I'd very much like your help."

"Great." She gave him a brilliant smile. "Let's start with your hat."

2

When Kieran had announced his reason for being in Wagon Train, Sara had resisted a powerful urge to hug him. So inappropriate. They'd just met.

But boy, had she wanted to grab hold and squeeze tight. Gorgeous, Irish and motherless, he was the most huggable man she'd met in ages.

Not to mention his accent. Although she hadn't been to Ireland yet, she'd probably get that opportunity next year. She'd coordinated a tour of New York City for a group from Dublin this past March and interacting with that bunch had been awesome. She could listen to those folks say *Dooblin* and *tat's craic* all day long.

None of them had looked like Kieran Haggerty, though. Lilting speech coming out of his mouth created all sorts of squishy reactions in her suddenly warm body. Did she have time to be his partner in this quest? Hell, yeah.

But first she'd help him find the right hat. "Do you know what size you wear?"

"Not really. I've worn adjustable caps all my life."

The way he said *adjoostable* made her toes curl. She took off the hat she had on and looked inside. "This is a seven and one-eighth. Want to try it, just for size?"

"All right." He set it lightly on his head, glanced in the full-length mirror and grinned. The hat perched a good two inches above the tips of his ears. "I look like an eejit."

"Eejit." She smiled back at him. "My Dublin tour group used that word all the time."

"You took a trip to Dublin?"

"No, the Dublin group came to New York and I organized a tour of the city for them. I had so much fun listening to them."

"That's what you do? Take folks around New York?" He handed over the hat.

"I'm not usually on the tour myself. I organize them, and not just for New York. I can plan a tour for most any large city in the country. The guide for the Dublin group's tour got sick at the last minute and we couldn't find a replacement so I stepped in."

"It's your company, then?"

She took it as a compliment that he imagined her capable of running the operation. "No, I work for Adventuring Travel."

His blue gaze sharpened. "I've seen buses in Dublin with that on the side."

"Those would be ours. We're world-wide, but I'm not trained on any international tours yet. I'll start next year. I can't wait for my turn to go to Dublin."

"My village isn't far from there. I'm in the city all the time. You'll have to ring me."

"I will. It's great to have local connections." And he'd just reminded her of the main reason to keep this relationship friendly but not too friendly. Different worlds, ships passing in the night and so on.

She put on her hat. Technically she didn't own it yet, but she would. "Since mine was a terrible fit, you'd better go up a size, or maybe two sizes. Are you familiar with the various brands?"

"Only Stetson."

"There are other options — Resistol, Justin, American Hat Company, you name it."

"I can see that." Hands thrust in the pockets of his jeans, he strolled the long wall, checking each display. "What's yours?"

"It's a Stetson." What a yummy guy. Long legs, easy gait, nice butt. She did her level best not to follow his every move, but it was a challenge. Clearly he wasn't trying to look sexy. He couldn't help it.

He paused by the Stetson display, surveyed the offerings and reached for a brown felt with a simple hatband. Holding it by the crown, he settled it on his head and tugged the brim down. Then he turned. "What do you think?"

She stared at him, awash in lust. The brim shaded his eyes just enough to add a touch of appealing mystery. The width of the hat drew attention to his broad shoulders and narrow hips.

His shirt and jeans resembled the clothes her brothers wore these days, and although his boots had laces, they still looked manly. He could easily pass for a cowboy. A hot one.

What did she think? If he walked out of Hannigan's wearing that hat he'd need a bodyguard to keep women at bay. She'd gladly accept the position. She'd seen him first.

"No good?" He reached to take it off.

"Oh, no. It's good. Very good. You just found yourself a hat on the first try. Congrats."

"It puts me in mind of the one Chuck Connors wore in *The Rifleman.*" He headed in her direction.

"I'll take your word for that."

"You didn't watch the show?" He checked his image in the mirror.

"It was before my time. Yours, too, for that matter."

"True." He made a slight adjustment to the tilt of the hat and turned back to her. "But Granny loves those old Westerns. Growing up I watched 'em all with her."

"Then I can't wait to introduce you to Desiree McLintock, the owner of the ranch where I'm staying."

"McLintock?" He brightened. "Like the name of the John Wayne film?"

"Exactly like that. She adores the movie, which is why she legally changed her name to McLintock."

"Amazing."

"Desiree's an original." Since he hadn't recognized the name M.R. Morrison, she might as well skip over that part of the story. "She named her place Rowdy Ranch after Rowdy Yates."

"Clint Eastwood. *Rawhide.*"

"Oh, yeah, you two will get along great. On top of it, she's lived here a long time, so she might have information on your mother."

"When do I get to meet this woman?"

"Maybe this afternoon. My folks are probably finished with their dessert by now and ready to drive back. They rented a five-person SUV when we flew in yesterday, so you could ride with us."

"But I've rented a room at the hotel, so I'll need a way to get—."

"I'll bring you back. As soon as we pay for our hats, we'll head over to the Buffalo."

"The Fluffy Buffalo?"

"That's the one. Everyone but me decided to order dessert after we finished lunch. I was more interested in getting a hat." And she was thrilled with how that choice had worked out.

"Could I get takeaway at the Buffalo?"

"I think so. You haven't eaten?"

"Not since early morning."

"Then you need food. And a pint."

"Listen to you, sounding Irish."

"Am I right about you wanting one?"

He chuckled. "You'd be right."

"They might even have Guinness." His soft chuckle had given her goosebumps. No question she was into him, but backing out of her offer wasn't an option. She'd just be careful.

"They do have Guinness. I saw it online."

"Okay, then. Here's the plan, if you're up for it. We'll walk over to the Buffalo, order your takeout, and while we're waiting you can have a pint. You can eat on the drive to the ranch. How does that sound?"

"Grand. I was knackered after the trip down here. And I'm that hungry my stomach thinks my throat's been cut."

"Then it's settled. Once my folks agree, which I know they will, I'll give Desiree a call to let her know we're bringing someone back with us, but I won't go into the details. That's better explained face-to-face."

"I agree. She'll be needing to look at the postcard and the picture."

"And you. I see the family resemblance in your face and hair. I can't tell eye color from the picture, but—"

"Green as shamrocks according to Granny. I got the blue from my father, who took off before I was born."

"I'm sorry."

"Not me. Granny says he was a bleedin' plonker. Never showed his face again. Good riddance." He said it casually, and the shadow of his hat muted any telltale emotion in his gaze.

Maybe he'd accepted being deserted by both his mother and his father, but she still wanted to hug him. In a comforting way. She didn't want to start anything that she couldn't finish.

Keep telling yourself that, girlfriend.

3

Kieran hadn't meant to bring up his shitehawk father, but the words had slipped out before he could stop them. Sara had a way of making him want to tell her things.

And when he did, the sympathy in her green eyes warmed his heart. Not that he needed any comforting where his father was concerned.

That said, he appreciated her kindness. Within minutes of arriving in Wagon Train he'd located a woman who was both stunning and compassionate. What were the chances of that?

Justine finished with her other customers and came to check on them. "Whoa, Kieran, that hat looks amazing on you."

"Thanks. I like it."

"I think we're both ready to check out." Sara swept a hand in his direction. "He hasn't eaten since early this morning so I suggested heading for the Buffalo."

"Then let's get you on your way." Justine turned and walked toward the register at the back of the shop. "I'll grab a couple of boxes."

"I'd like to skip the box," Kieran said as he and Sara followed her. "I'll wear my hat on the plane home or keep it in my lap." He wouldn't trust it to a box in an overhead bin. He'd seen how folks crammed their luggage in.

"I don't need one either, Justine. I'll do the same as Kieran when I fly back."

"Alrighty, then." Justine stepped behind the counter. "Who's going first?"

He gestured Sara to go ahead of him while he dug out his wallet. He'd noted the price of the hat before he'd tried it on. Probably shouldn't have reached for it, but it was exactly what he'd had in mind. Sure enough, the fit was perfect and Sara liked it.

He'd be using a credit card, but no getting 'round it. The hat was dear, way over budget. Maybe he'd skip a few meals to make up for this splurge.

Then it was his turn to pay and Justine told him he owed even more. "Did the price go up?"

"That's including tax."

"Oh." He hesitated. It wasn't much in comparison to the entire cost, but the surprise of it snapped him back to reality. He'd established a saving habit early in his life, which was the only reason he was standing here. Was he an eejit for buying this hat?

"Irish citizens don't pay sales tax," Sara said gently. "I learned that from my Dublin tour group."

And he could just hear them complaining. He didn't want to give Sara the impression he was tight as two coats of paint. "The tax is fine. It's only a wee bit more, after all." He studied the machine on the counter. "Looks like I just slide—"

"Wait." Justine reached over and blocked the machine with her hand. "Let me check something. The other day Eddie made a spreadsheet of everything we're including in our pre-Labor Day sale."

"Isn't that in May?"

"Not in this country." Sara glanced at him. "We have a different date than you do."

"And it's coming up." Justine took a sheet of paper from a shelf under the register. "If your hat's on the list..." She scanned the contents. "It most certainly is." She tapped some buttons on the register and he suddenly had a sizable discount.

Suspicious as hell. "When does the sale start?"

"Soon enough that I'm fine with giving you the sales price."

He met her gaze. She was hedging with that answer and likely stretching the truth, but arguing the point would be ungrateful. "Thank you."

"My pleasure. Now you two vamoose. I'll be in touch if my folks know anything."

"I appreciate it and thank you for the discount." Before he turned away he tipped his hat.

"Oh, my." Justine fanned herself. "You have the makings of a cowboy, Kieran."

"Thanks." He was laughing as he and Sara went out the door. "Good thing she's never seen me on a horse."

"You don't know how to ride one?"

"Never had the opportunity." He fell into step beside her as they walked down the footpath toward the Fluffy Buffalo. He adjusted his stride, changing to more of a saunter, like Chuck Connors might have looked on his way to the local pub.

"Maybe you'll have a chance to get on a horse while you're on this trip."

"There's a stable in town?" He hadn't thought to include that in the budget.

"Not that I know of, but I might be able to arrange something out at Rowdy Ranch. They have a lot of horses."

"Is it one of those dude ranches, then?" He'd heard they were expensive. Likely he couldn't afford their rates.

"No, just a sprawling family setup. We came into the mix when my brother Dallas moved here and became friends with one of Desiree's nine sons."

"*Nine*?"

"And one daughter. Desiree loves kids."

"Her husband must love 'em, too."

"He does, but... no, I'm not going into that now. Long story short, Dallas married Desiree's daughter and my brother Trent also moved here. He's married a local woman and they're expecting a baby. My parents, my sister and I flew in yesterday."

"Do you like it here?"

"For visits, sure. It's fun pretending to be a cowgirl. That's why I wanted the hat."

"Looks good on you."

"I could say the same about your hat. You'd pass for a cowboy until you open your mouth."

"Can't do much about how I talk."

"I wouldn't want you to. Your accent is charming."

"Is it, now?" He'd never considered his way of speaking as an asset. "Why is that?"

"There's a lilt to your voice and a way you brush past consonants that's very appealing."

"If you say so." In other words, she enjoyed listening to him. He'd take it.

"But you don't sound like a cowboy. It would help if you sprinkled a few *yes, ma'ams* and *no, ma'ams* into the conversation. Assuming you're talking to a woman, of course."

"Why would I do that?"

"It's considered polite. The cowboys around here use that phrase a lot."

"Where I come from, a woman doesn't like it when you call her *ma'am*. It's insulting, like you think she's old."

"That's not the case here. The McLintock men say it all the time."

"To you?"

"Sure."

"Even though you're so young?"

"I'm twenty-six." She lifted her chin a notch.

He smiled. "Still too young to be called *ma'am*."

She waited for a lorry to drive past before they crossed the street. "Ah, but if they say it with a twinkle in their eyes, it's adorable. If they add enthusiasm, like *yes, ma'am!* you know they're excited about whatever you've suggested. Then there's slow and sexy, like *yeess, maaa-aaam.* That delivery can be extremely seductive."

"Not in Ireland."

"I believe you, but in cowboy country, that phrase is the secret sauce." She headed across the street.

He kept pace with her. "I see."

"If it's a stretch for you, since you've been taught the opposite, then never mind. And here we are." She walked toward the Buffalo's front entrance.

He beat her to it, grabbing the brass handle and swinging the door wide.

She glanced up, amusement in her eyes. "You must be ready for lunch."

He chuckled. "Yes, ma'am."

Her eyes widened and her cheeks flushed. "Well, done, cowboy."

The flash of arousal in her gaze wasn't lost on him. Secret sauce, indeed.

4

Teaching Kieran the benefits of saying *yes, ma'am* had been a tactical error. Sara's pulse was still racing as she walked past the large wooden buffalo and tripped the sensors. The buffalo moaned *Hot enouuuuf for youuuu?*"

A little too hot, thank you, and she wasn't talking about the weather. She glanced toward the table where her folks and Lani were giving her the eye. She waved.

"What the devil?" Kieran stared at the mascot in obvious fascination, backed up and came through again. Then he started laughing. "That's gas."

If she hadn't spent time with the Dublin group, she wouldn't know *that's gas* meant he thought the talking buffalo was hilarious. His reaction to it had likely drawn her family's attention, too, especially since the mid-afternoon crowd in the Buffalo was sparse.

She glanced toward their table and sure enough, Lani and her parents were focused on her unexpected companion. She turned back to him. "Liked that, did you?"

"Loved it. What else does it say? That can't be the only thing."

"They change it up for each holiday, but since August doesn't have one, I guess weather makes a good topic. Supposedly it's hot for this time of year. Anyway, we should go—"

"Who have we here, Sara?" Cecily, senior member of the wait staff, hurried over, menu in hand. "I don't believe I know this gentleman."

"He's Kieran Haggerty from Ireland."

"Seriously?"

"Seriously. Kieran, meet Cecily, the best server I've ever encountered. Incredible memory."

Kieran whipped off his hat and offered his hand. "How are you... ma'am?"

Sara pressed her lips together to keep from giggling.

"I'm just dandy, thank you, Kieran. Welcome to Wagon Train."

"He was in Hannigan's to buy a hat, just like me. Flew into Missoula this morning and drove down. I brought him over to meet my folks and get some food."

"Then take a look at the menu, son." She handed it over. "See if anything strikes your fancy. I'll get it started while you go socialize."

"The egg salad sandwich looks good."

"Is it possible we could get it to go?" Her family was probably ready to leave and she was eager for this meeting between Kieran and Desiree. "I'd like him to ride out to the ranch with us, but I never asked if you do takeout."

"Absolutely, and you'll love Rowdy Ranch, son. I'll put in your order. Would you like a pint of Guinness while you wait for it?"

"Yes, ma'am."

He was a quick study, this Irishman.

"I'll bring it to the table. You'd better scamper on over there, Sara, girl. Your sister just got to her feet. Looks like she's ready to find out what's what."

"Thanks, Cecily. I see her." Lani was on her way, brown curls bouncing on her shoulders, a polite smile on her lips and *what-the-hell?* in her eyes. "Hey, Lani, this is Kieran Haggerty from Ireland."

She blinked. "Ireland?" Astonishment replaced her big sister's protective expression.

"Yes, ma'am." Kieran held out his hand. "How are you?"

"I'm fine, thanks. What brings you to—"

"We met when he came into Hannigan's looking for a hat. He has quite a story. After hearing it I decided he needs to talk with Desiree."

"What story?"

"Let's go sit. Mom and Dad need to hear it, too."

When they reached the table, she introduced her parents as Vanessa and Harry. Kieran used his newfound *ma'am* on her mother, which made her smile, but she would have been okay with Vanessa. New Jersey residents weren't steeped in the tradition the way folks were out here.

Her dad grabbed an extra chair and they made room for Kieran at the table between Sara and Lani. Cecily brought a mug of dark beer for Kieran and refilled everyone's water glass. Satisfied that they didn't need anything more, she collected the dessert plates and left.

Kieran hooked his hat carefully on the back of his chair, took a sip of his beer and launched into his explanation. Her sister and parents listened with almost identical expressions of sadness and sympathy, as if they had the same reaction she'd had, to draw him into a big hug.

When he showed them the postcard and photograph he didn't pass them around or get them anywhere near his Guinness. Then he tucked them away in his shirt pocket and picked up his beer. "And that's why I came to Wagon Train."

Her dad cleared his throat. "And your father?"

"Not in the picture." He took another swallow of Guinness. "It's just been me and Granny since Grandpa died. She didn't want me to come, but if I could put her mind to rest... and mine, for that matter, I'd be willing to do most anything for that."

"I think he needs to talk to Desiree," Sara said. "He has a rental and could follow us out, but he's probably still jet lagged. If he comes with us, he'll have a chance to eat his sandwich on the way. I can bring him back here later."

"Or I could just follow you out." Kieran turned to her. "I can handle the drive."

"While eating a sandwich?"

"Well...."

"Ride out with us, son," her dad said. "We have multiple people who can bring you back, including me. Where are you staying?"

"The Wagon Train Hotel."

"That's nice," her mom said. "Historic."

When her mom and dad exchanged a glance, Sara had no trouble interpreting it. There were rooms available in the kids' wing of Rowdy Ranch, but it wasn't their place to say so. Desiree probably would, though.

"Desiree will be a good resource." Her mom focused on Kieran. "She was here back then and I get the impression she's been active in the community from the beginning."

"Hey, guys, what about Andy?" Lani said. "He's been here a long time, too, and putting out a newspaper. If Kieran's mother..." She faltered and sent Kieran an apologetic look. "I mean, newspapers keep track of...."

"When someone dies." His voice was steady as he finished Lani's sentence. "And she must have. Like I said, she was faithful about those postcards, one a week. She wouldn't have stopped sending them unless something happened to her."

"It's brave of you to come looking for answers, son." Her dad eyed Kieran with respect. "Rowdy Ranch is a good place to start. Besides Desiree and Andy, there's Buck and Marybeth, the couple who've been helping Desiree with the ranch and the kids for more than thirty years. Out of those four, surely someone has information."

"Here's your egg salad sandwich." Cecily arrived with a paper bag folded down at the top. "I put in some chips and a couple of cookies."

"And we have water bottles in the car," Lani added.

He stood and pulled out his wallet. "I appreciate it. What do I—"

"Put it on our tab, please, Cecily." Her dad got to his feet. "The beer, too."

"No, no." Kieran turned to him. "That's kind of you, but I can—"

"Of course you can. But we want to help. Buying your lunch would make us happy."

Kieran glanced at her.

"Just go with it." She pushed back her chair. "Make my family happy."

"Then thank you, all of you. I'll be telling Granny I was treated like a king while I was in Wagon Train."

"Then we're outta here." Her dad picked up the bill and stepped away from the table. "I'll take care of this and meet you guys at the front door."

"Thanks, Dad." She gave him a quick hug.

"You're welcome, sweetie."

She slung her purse over her shoulder and met Kieran's gaze. "Ready to leave?"

He had a teasing gleam in his eyes. "Yes—"

"Never mind. Let's go."

His soft chuckle as he followed her toward the door made her tingle all over. She should never have suggested that routine, never have handed him a seductive technique that might be her undoing.

Luckily he'd only used it when they were in public. If he ever deployed that tactic when they were alone, she wouldn't be responsible for her actions.

5

Kieran admired Harry Armstrong's confidence as he switched on the engine and backed out of a space in front of the Buffalo. Seemed like they were way too close to the lorry parked next to them.

He braced for the screech of metal on metal, but it never came. They cleared the spot and rolled down Main Street without hitting anything.

Sitting in the back seat was slightly less disorienting than being behind the wheel. But he still couldn't get used to looking to his right and seeing the edge of the road. It was too close. They'd veer off into a ditch any second.

Sara had taken the middle seat next to him and Lani sat by the left-side door. Tucked in thigh-to-thigh with Sara gave him ideas he shouldn't be having, but it was either focus on her lovely profile or the unsettling landscape whizzing by on the wrong side of the vehicle. He looked at Sara.

Extracting her mobile from the handbag on her lap, she called Desiree to announce they were bringing someone back with them and hoping she'd be available to meet him.

He could only hear her end of the call and was surprised at the wee amount of detail she gave Desiree — only that he'd just arrived in town and desperately needed this meeting. Sara didn't even mention he was from Ireland.

Tucking her phone away, she glanced at him. "She's looking forward to it."

"The mystery man?"

"That's on purpose. If you want her attention, give her a puzzle to solve."

Vanessa laughed. "Isn't that the truth."

"But you didn't even tell her my name."

"Kieran isn't a name you hear all the time. Pair it up with Haggerty and she'd ask if you're Irish, and then if you're from Ireland, and then—"

"Before you know what hit you, she's wormed out the whole story," Vanessa said. "We've all learned that about Desiree. She's curious and she's persistent. Since this isn't a conversation to have over the phone, Sara was smart to limit the info."

"We're lucky she's not on deadline," Lani said.

"Only because she burned the midnight oil before we arrived," Harry said. "She told me it was down to the wire, but fortunately the characters cooperated and helped her write the ending."

"Desiree's a writer?"

"Bingo. Remember when I asked if you were here to see M.R. Morrison, the author?"

"I do."

"That's Desiree's pen name. Until recently, readers believed she was a man. She took that name because when she published her first book thirty-five years ago, all the popular Western writers were men. Her publisher thought nobody would buy a woman's Western stories."

"That's why she loves old Western films and TV shows? Because she writes about the West?"

"It's more the other way around," Harry said. "She was into those shows as a kid and had the urge to write stories like that. She's built a successful career out of it, too."

"While raising ten children?"

"That's where Buck and Marybeth come in." Sara got out her mobile. "Let me show you some pictures I took at Dallas's wedding last February. This is Marybeth. She was Angie's matron of honor."

He gazed at the seventy-something lady who'd fastened her gray braids into a crown and decorated it with flowers. Joy shone in her eyes and in her wide smile. Made his chest hurt. Granny hadn't worn an expression like that in years. "Nice."

"And here are the McLintock brothers all lined up waiting for the wedding to start. That's our brother Dallas and next to him is Trent, our other brother, who was his best man."

"'Tis a massive group, there. Nine of 'em. Bet nobody messes with those fellas."

"They're completely harmless."

"I wouldn't put it that way," Harry said. "They aren't likely to start something, but Marsh is into kickboxing and all of them are in excellent shape. If they need to defend themselves or a loved one, they won't hesitate."

"I can't picture Rance duking it out with someone, though," Sara said. "First he'd try to relieve the tension with a joke."

"He might, at that. He's a character."

Lani snorted. "That's one way to put it."

"Which one is Rance?"

"This one." Sara pointed to the next to the last in the lineup. "He and Lucky, the one at the end, are the same age, the two youngest boys. Rance is Desiree's biological son and Lucky was adopted. I haven't heard the story behind that. Mom, have you?"

"I haven't. When I heard they were the same age, I assumed they were fraternal twins since they don't look alike. Then somebody told me Lucky's adopted, but that's all I know."

"Oh, well. Not important right now. Here's one of Desiree and her husband Andy, although at the time they weren't married yet."

"Then he's not the father of that lot?"

"No, he—"

"Ah, their father died, then." He studied the handsome copper-haired woman in the photograph.

The fella was looking at her like she was the last biscuit on the plate, while she smiled at the person taking the picture — who would be Sara. He saw confidence in her eyes and strength in her posture. "I'll wager she doesn't put up with plonkers."

Vanessa chuckled. "I can guess what a plonker is and you're right. She doesn't put up with them. When she's in the room, there's no doubt who's in charge."

Sara leaned toward the front seat. "Mom, should we tell him about the fathers?"

"*Sar*-a." Lani sighed. "You can't say something like that and *not* tell him."

He rose to her defense. "Yes, she can. If it's best not to tell me, then don't worry about it, Sara."

She glanced back at him. "It's just that you're under the impression there was only one father."

"And I know better, now. You said *fathers,* which tells me she had more than one husband, not counting the current one. Now the ten children make more sense."

"She didn't have any husbands. Not until Andy."

"None? Then how did she—"

"Let me handle this." Vanessa twisted around in her seat so she could make eye contact with him. "Desiree loved the idea of kids but had issues with marriage. She chose men who weren't keen on tying the knot and would give her custody of the child they conceived together."

That set him back. "Nine different fellas?"

"Seven. She has a set of twins and one of the men fathered two boys about a year apart."

"And they all disappeared once they'd done the deed?"

"Only one cut off contact. Two passed away. The other four have kept in touch with their kids and last I heard, three of them have moved back to Wagon Train so they can be closer to the family now that grandchildren are being born."

"That...." He shook his head. "I've never heard of anything so...."

"Hard to imagine?"

He nodded. "Makes my head explode."

"And here's the kicker. Despite her non-traditional lifestyle, she's a pillar of the community, admired by everyone. The McLintocks are the most respected family in Wagon Train."

"Amazing."

"Even more incredible, her bestselling books were essential to her pulling it off, but until a couple of weeks ago, only her immediate family and a small group of female friends knew that she's M.R. Morrison."

"Why unmask herself now?"

"I think you should ask her. I might not get it right. Everything I just told you is fact. Her reasons for going public with her writing identity... those are hers to tell."

"I feel like I'm about to meet a legend."

"That's not far off, son," Harry said.

His gaze locked with Sara's. "What did you get me into?"

"Nothing you can't handle, cowboy."

He liked the way she was looking at him. Liked it a lot. If they were in County Kildare, he'd know what that look meant.

But he was a stranger in a strange land. Before he made a fool of himself, he needed to find out what was going on with her.

Was she the type who enjoyed stirring up a fella but never intended to follow through on the invitation she'd issued? He didn't believe it. She'd been nothing but kind to him. Her wish to help him find out about his mum was sincere.

But if she wanted the sort of thing from him that her eyes were communicating, had she thought it through? After this week they'd likely never see each other again.

That truth was only the beginning of the mess they could make of this. Then came the logistics of the situation. She was staying out here within arm's reach of her relations.

He had privacy to offer in the form of his hotel room, but she had no transportation unless she used the family rental. He couldn't picture her asking to borrow that vehicle so she could spend the night with him at the hotel.

Even if she was sassy enough to ask, her family would likely remind her that this was a dead-end situation. And they would be right.

But what if she didn't care about that? What if she was all for living in the moment and capturing joy wherever she found it? If that was the case, where did he stand on the matter?

He didn't know. Such a circumstance had never presented itself. Living in one spot all his life, he'd never been in the position of wanting a woman he'd never see again. He saw his ex-girlfriends all the bleedin' time.

Lani leaned forward so she could see past Sara. "Don't forget about your sandwich."

"Oh, right." He picked up the bag he'd set between his feet to keep it from tipping.

"I'll get you some water from the back." Sara unlatched her belt and scooted around so she could kneel on the seat and reach in the back. Moments later she handed him a chilled bottle.

He decided against saying *thank you, ma'am* and settled for just *thanks.* After this meeting with Desiree, however it went, he and Sara would have a talk.

6

As they all exited the SUV in the parking area a few yards away from Desiree's ranch house, Lani pulled Sara aside and lowered her voice. "What are you doing?"

"Nothing." She boldly met Lani's gaze, but inside a little voice whispered *liar, liar, pants on fire.*

"He's only here for a week."

"So?"

"Why are you flirting with him?"

She folded like a cheap shoji screen. "Because I'm an eejit."

"A what?"

"Never mind. You're right. I'll—"

"Are you girls coming?" their mom called out.

"Be right there, Mom," Sara called back. "Lani saw something stuck in my teeth."

"Because you're lying through them," Lani muttered as they walked toward the group of three standing by the porch steps. "I thought you liked Rance?"

"I do. He's funny. But Kieran... gets to me."

"Obviously."

"Anyway, I can't like Rance."

"Why not?"

"You like him."

"No, I don't."

"Now who's lying through her teeth?"

"Go to hell, Sara."

"Love you, too, sis." Then she flashed her parents a smile. "Sorry to hold up the parade. It was a sesame seed from my hamburger bun. Sneaky little critters."

Her mother gave her a look, clearly not believing a word of it. She probably had the urge to deliver the same message Lani just had.

"Maybe someone should check my teeth," Kieran said. "My sandwich was on a bun with seeds."

"Let me look." She offered way too fast, but damned if she was turning that job over to someone else. She'd stop flirting, but she was still his sidekick. "Smile."

A twinkle in his blue eyes, he obliged, putting her right back under his spell.

She quickly examined those pearly whites and did her best to ignore his sensual, kissable mouth. A faint shadow darkened his upper lip. He'd clearly found a moment to shave before making the drive from Missoula, but he'd have some prickles by nightfall. She longed to find out firsthand. "You're fine."

"Then let's go in," her dad said. He started toward the porch steps. "She knows we're here. Sam just barked."

"I thought I heard a dog!" Kieran lit up. "What kind is he?"

"A collie," her dad said. "The spitting image of Lassie."

"Yeah? Collies are my—"

Before he could finish the sentence, Desiree appeared clutching Sam's collar. "Hi, there. He heard a new voice and can't wait to make another friend."

Kieran moved forward eagerly. "Wouldya mind turnin' him loose? I used to have—"

"You're Irish!" Desiree grinned as she let go of Sam, who made a beeline for Kieran.

"That I am. Born and bred." Nudging back his hat, he crouched down and embraced the collie, burying his fingers in the dog's silky ruff. "Hey, Sam. Hey, boyo. You're a beauty, aren't you, now?"

Sam wiggled with joy and made little moaning sounds of ecstasy.

Desiree came down the steps, her brow furrowed, as she gazed at her visitor. "What's your name, son?"

He glanced up. "Kieran Haggerty. From County Kildare. Just arrived today."

Her frown deepened. "How old are you?"

"Just turned thirty-two." He slowly rose to his feet and took off his hat.

"You remind me of someone."

"I do?"

She stared at him for several uncomfortable seconds. "Why are you here, Kieran?" There was a faint tremor in her voice.

Sara went on alert. Desiree was famous for keeping her cool, but judging from that tremor and her troubled expression, she was on the verge of losing it.

"I'm looking to find out what happened to my mum. She was here thirty—"

With a soft cry, Desiree covered her mouth.

He stiffened. "You know?"

She nodded, tears in her eyes. "Come... come inside."

Sara's heart pounded. Whatever had Desiree this rattled had to be a very big deal. As they all trooped into the house, Lani grabbed her hand and squeezed. Her mom and dad exchanged a worried glance.

Desiree led the way down the hall to the living room. "Sit wherever you..." She swallowed. "Wherever you want." She murmured something to her dog, then gestured toward the large leather sofa and the armchairs that flanked it. Her gaze never left Kieran.

He took a ragged breath. "I'd as soon stand."

"Me... me, too." She pressed a hand to her chest.

They all stood, as if sitting would be disrespectful considering that something big was coming.

Digging in her pocket, Desiree pulled out a tissue and mopped her face. "Well, then." She balled the tissue in her fist. "I knew your mother. Your mum."

His face paled. "She's dead, isn't she?"

"Yes, but—"

"I knew she was, but a part of me wanted to believe...."

"I'm sorry." She took a quick breath. "There's more, Kieran. You have—" She gulped. "You have a half-brother."

Lucky. Sara gasped.

Kieran went white.

Sara lunged forward and grabbed his arm as he swayed. "I've got you." Crazy thing to say. If he went down, she'd go with him.

He didn't acknowledge her support, just stood there shaking and breathing fast, too fast. She took his hat from his unresisting fingers.

Her mom sprang into action. "I'll get some water."

Desiree went to him and gripped his shoulders.

Good. With two of them bracing him, he'd stay upright.

"I shouldn't have blurted it out." Desiree's voice quivered. "I should have waited, led up to it. I—"

"A brother." The faint words barely made it past his lips.

"His name's Lucky. Born the same day as Rance."

"What... what happened?"

"She... your mother wasn't strong. It was... too much."

His breath hitched and his jaw flexed as he looked past Desiree into a distant past. "Was she... did anybody...."

"She had a proper burial. And a stone."

His eyes closed and he managed a gruff *thank you*. His chest heaved and he refocused on

Desiree. "Granny will be... that means a lot to us. To me."

"Your granny? Jane's mother?"

"Jane?"

"It was the name she gave us." She began gently massaging his shoulders.

Sara stepped back. This was a time for mothering, and Desiree was clearly a pro at that, even under stress.

So was her mom, who came in with a glass of water and gently pressed it into Kieran's hand. He gulped it down, thanked her and handed it back.

"I'll take you to the cemetery when you're ready." Desiree's voice was steady but husky with emotion. "Clearly the right name isn't on that stone."

"It's Freya." He cleared the hoarseness from his throat. "Freya Noreen Haggerty."

"She called herself Jane Smith."

Anger brought a flush to his pale cheeks. "She married that shitehawk Ronny Smith?"

"No. I doubt that was his name, anyway. I never met him. He was long gone when your mom went into labor."

"You spoke to her?"

"For most of an afternoon. When I heard she was alone, I asked if we could share a room until one of us was ready to deliver."

"Did she... mention me?"

The vulnerability in that question made Sara's throat hurt.

"She didn't say anything about her past."

"Nothing?"

"I think she was ashamed to find herself in such a fix. She didn't want word getting back to her family."

"But her postcards were... she sounded so happy."

"Of course she'd write happy things. She knew she'd made a terrible mistake, but she told me she had plans to turn things around. If she'd lived, I would have helped her."

He let out a groan of frustration. "If only she'd let Granny and Grandpa know the truth!"

"Would you have?"

He was silent for a moment. "No."

"I'll have the stone redone."

"I'll pay for it."

Desiree opened her mouth, then closed it again.

Sara recognized that maneuver. Desiree wouldn't argue the matter now, but etching the correct name on the headstone would turn out to be a bargain, just like Justine had given him one for his hat.

"That fecking Ronny Smith." The steel was back in his voice and his blue eyes flashed. "Do you think he's still alive? If I could track that bastard down, I'd—"

"I tried, mostly for Lucky's sake. Couldn't find a trace of him. Men like him don't usually live very long."

"May he rot in hell."

"I'm sure he will."

As his anger slowly faded, he dragged in a breath. "And I have a *brother*." He might as well have said he had a unicorn judging from the level of disbelief in his tone.

"Yes."

"That's... I can't even...."

"I know."

He turned to Sara. "You have that picture on your mobile. Can I see it, please?"

"Coming up." She took it out of her purse and scrolled until she found the wedding shot. Then she enlarged it to give him a closeup of Lucky before she handed over her phone.

He studied the picture for a long time, as if looking at it would cement the idea in his brain. "He has her green eyes." He sounded wistful and a little jealous.

"But you have her mouth," Desiree said. "I wouldn't have thought I'd remember that, but I do. And her cheekbones. You both got those." She hesitated. "This will be huge for Lucky, just like it is for you, but I don't want to rush you into...."

"Where is he?" He continued to stare at the image on the phone.

"Down at the bookstore with Oksana."

"And she's...."

"His wife and business partner. If you'd shown up last week, they would have been at the new location in Apple Grove, but they're here this week. Do you want me to drive you to town so you can meet him?"

"Thank you, but... not yet." He squared his shoulders, his expression resolute. "After he closes up shop is better." He handed Sara her phone with a murmur of thanks. "If someone can please run me back before closing time, I'll wait at the hotel until—"

"You have a room there?"

"I do. And a rented vehicle. Sara's folks were kind enough to bring me out, but once I get used to driving on the wrong side, I'll be able to take care of myself just fine."

"I can tell you're used to that."

"I am."

"And maybe you'd prefer the hotel, but... you're family. I would very much like you to stay out here with us. Will you consider it?"

He didn't answer right away. After an audible swallow he ducked his head. Then he drew a deep breath and looked up, his eyes moist. "I'd be honored."

"Thank you." She drew him into a hug.

He hugged her back, his eyes squeezed tight.

The emotions crowding Sara's chest threatened to spill out, but she didn't want to add to the drama. She blinked away her tears and stared at the floor.

She'd promised Lani she'd dial back her natural response to Kieran, but that wouldn't be easy. He'd captured her imagination from the get-go. Now he'd stolen her heart.

7

Overwhelmed. Kieran had never been more disoriented in his life. He'd prepared himself for learning his mum was gone. Or he thought he had.

Maybe a fella couldn't prepare for such a thing. Hearing it from someone who'd been there should have made it easier. Instead it was more vivid, more heartbreaking to find out she'd been so alone at the end.

Not completely alone, though. She'd had the brief comfort of the woman he was clinging to like a life raft on a storm-tossed sea. He finally made himself let go of Desiree, hoping to God he didn't break down in front of all these people. In front of Sara.

Of the lot of them, he was most comfortable with her, had been ever since their time in Hannigan's. What would she think of him now that she'd seen him like this, all choked up and on the brink of losing his shit?

Screwing up his courage, he glanced around at the five people in the room, each of them gazing at him with sympathy. He ended with Sara. "I'll be honest. I'm having trouble handling...." He waved a hand in the air, unable to put the rest of it into words.

She came to his rescue. "Anybody would. I'm guessing you could use some down time."

He grasped that welcome straw. "Yeah, like a walk or something. But I don't know the lay of the land."

"Tell you what. I'll go with you, but I won't say a single word." She handed over his hat. "I'll just make sure you don't get lost. I'll be your guide dog."

Despite his inner turmoil, that concept made him smile. And gave him another idea. He looked at Desiree. "Can we take Sam?"

"Of course."

"Where'd he go?" He'd lost track of the collie when Desiree had started to cry.

"He's here. Sam, come."

He appeared, trotting around the furniture, tail wagging.

"Where was he?"

"On his bed over by the fireplace. You can't see it from here. I sent him over there when we first came in."

"Missed that." He held out his hand to Sam. "Wanna go for a walk, boyo?"

Sam's ears shot up and he danced in place.

Desiree smiled. "That's a yes."

"Then let's go." Kieran motioned toward the door and glanced at Sara. "Ready?"

She nodded, and true to her word, stayed silent as they followed Sam down the hall. Put him in mind of Granny's saying — *A silent mouth is sweet to hear.*

But he wouldn't care if she wanted to share her thoughts. She must have some. "You can talk, you know."

She shook her head.

"Suit yourself." He opened the door. Sam, who'd obviously been taught to be a gentleman, waited for Sara to exit first.

He motioned to the dog. "Go on with you, Sam."

The collie bounded out and down the steps to join Sara. She paused and glanced back, waiting for him.

He couldn't think of any face he'd rather see right now than hers. Her bright spirit calmed him in ways he couldn't explain. He just liked looking at her, being with her.

The minute he closed the door behind him, he exhaled. As he crossed the porch, tension slipped from his shoulders and the knot in his chest loosened. "That's better."

She gave him an understanding smile that said more than any words. Maybe they didn't have to talk, after all.

At the top of the steps he took a quick survey of the peaceful scene in front of him. A red hip-roofed barn sat off to the left and a pasture of grazing horses lay straight ahead, although it was farther away than the barn.

Beyond the stretch of pasture, a stand of pines glowed velvet green in the afternoon sun. To his right, the dirt road they'd come in on made a slight bend to the left and disappeared. Any direction she chose was fine with him.

Clattering down the steps, he put on his hat. "When did you take charge of my hat?"

She shrugged.

"Good thing you did. I might have mangled it."

Sam pranced around them, his tongue hanging out.

"Looks like Sam's getting impatient. Lead the way."

Adjusting the fit of her hat, Sara took off in the general direction of the barn. He fell into step on her right and Sam took her left, keeping pace with her, his head high, his ears at attention.

Sara had kept her hat on ever since she'd bought it, whether she'd been indoors or out. Come to think of it, Irish women sometimes did that, too. He'd automatically taken his off because that's what he would have done before going into Granny's house.

Granny. She'd be asleep by now. That was a blessing. He'd have time to plan how he'd break the news. He couldn't predict how she'd take it. Hell, he couldn't predict his own behavior going forward, let alone someone else's.

But stretching his legs felt good. Breathing fresh country air cleared his head a little. Walking beside Sara reassured him. Although he barely knew her, they'd fallen into a natural friendship that he found steadying. He had the impulse to take her hand. Decided against it.

Granny believed in fairies and omens and Fate with a capital F. He swore he didn't, that it was all nonsense, but this trip had him questioning... well, everything.

As they drew closer to the barn, a footpath revealed itself to the right side of it. Looked like the trail ran along the pasture fence and on toward the pines.

Sure enough, when they got beyond the barn the view opened up, giving him a good look at the massive Sapphire Mountains to the west. According to his online research, sapphires were still mined there.

He glanced past Sara to the horses nibbling on grass only a few feet from the fence. They paid no attention to the dog or the humans.

He'd never had much chance to look at horses before. These were beautiful, their coats glossy, their manes falling gracefully along the curve of their powerful necks. Different colors, too — brown, black and white, gold, gray, even a white one that looked like the Lone Ranger's horse Silver.

Lucky had grown up with these animals. One of those in the pasture might be his. He'd landed in a bed of clover, thanks to his mum being in the hospital at the same time as Desiree. And that fine woman had the generosity to adopt a motherless child.

Once he told Granny about that, she'd add more candles, one for Lucky and one for Desiree. That much he knew. And she'd cry. If only he could be there with her, but he wasn't keeping this to himself until he flew home. She deserved to hear it quickly, just not in the middle of the night.

As they left the pasture behind, Sam dashed down the well-traveled path. Evidently he knew this route and the many exciting spots requiring investigation along the way.

The collie reminded him so much of Bailey, who'd loved trips to the outskirts of town where he could roam and sniff to his heart's content. "I miss having a dog."

Sara glanced up, eyebrows raised in a clear invitation to expand on that subject.

"His name was Bailey, a collie like Sam but slightly different coloring. Not a purebred, for sure. Had him when I was a lad and oh, did we have the adventures. I was eighteen when he got sick and died."

She reached over and squeezed his arm.

He liked that, liked it a little too much. He'd pictured them working together to solve the mystery of his mother's disappearance. Wouldn't need to do that, now, would they?

Instead he'd spend the week getting to know his brother, which wouldn't leave much time to get to know Sara. He'd planned to have a talk with her about her intentions toward him. Likely her intentions had changed in the past hour. Like everything else.

What had he been talking about? Oh, yeah. His dog. "I was in a state when I lost Bailey, but the truth is once I started learning a trade and working steady, I wouldn't have had time for him."

She cocked her head to one side and looked at him. Easy to figure out she wanted more on the subject of his work, which he hadn't mentioned before.

"Carpentry. I'm in construction back home. Most of the jobs are in Dublin. Takes a lot of petrol, which cuts into my earnings. I'd move there, but Granny would hate living in the city and I can't leave her. Not sure I'd care for city life, either, if it comes to that."

Sam had found a stick. He trotted back with it in his mouth and dropped it in the middle of the path, leaving them to decide who'd play with him.

"Want to throw it?"

She shook her head.

"Alrighty, then." He scooped up the stick and looked it over. The bark was gone, leaving a smooth wood that shouldn't easily splinter. "You found a good one, Sam. Go get it!" He sent the stick flying toward the trees.

Sam retrieved it in no time, so he kept up the game until they were so close to the trees that throwing it made no sense. "Game's over, Sam." He shoved the stick in his back pocket. "That was fun, though. Brings back memories."

As they stepped into the cool shade of the pines, he looked over at Sara. "I appreciate your decision to stay quiet and let me ramble on, but I'd really like to know more about Lucky. Since we're alone, I can get your version as an unprejudiced observer."

"That makes sense. Keep in mind this is only my second time here and I haven't seen much of him since we flew in."

"But you were here for your brother's wedding, when you took those pictures."

"Yes, and Lucky was in the middle of a huge drama that week. Based on what I gathered from Rance, it was mostly because his mixed-up brother had his head up his ass."

He chuckled. "That doesn't sound good."

"Long story short, he had the hots for Oksana but didn't think he was good enough for her. He came to his senses, though. I think his family had a lot to do with that, although that's just an educated guess. They don't talk about it."

"Do you think the circumstances of his birth bothered him?"

"Again, I don't know for sure, but it's logical. Anyway, Oksana took him back and they're madly in love."

"I've struggled with not feeling good enough. My father's a plonker and my mum ran off and left me. But Granny and Grandpa treated me like I was pure gold. Granny still does. That's helped."

"You are pure gold."

That brought him to a dead stop. "What?"

"A poet named Maya Angelou said *When someone shows you who they are, believe them the first time.*"

"I think I've heard that, but—"

"You've shown me who you are. You're brave, strong and persistent. You care about others. You're the real deal, Kieran. I'm just sad we won't... that we can't...."

"Me, too." Shoving aside all the voices in his head telling him it was a mistake, he reached for her.

She didn't resist when he pulled her close, but she didn't nestle against him either. Instead of winding her arms around his neck, she laid her palms against his chest. "We shouldn't."

"I know." Taking off his hat, he dipped his head under the brim of hers. "But I'm not as strong as you think." Surrendering to a yearning deep in his soul, he kissed her.

_8_

Kieran's velvet lips rested gently against Sara's before gradually increasing the pressure. She could still pull away, still call a halt to this madness. But his mouth felt exactly the way she'd known it would. _Wonderful._

He tasted of spicy mustard, a flavor she happened to love, and he... oh, yeah, this Irishman knew how to kiss. He didn't rush it, but there was nothing tentative about his approach.

He wanted in, and she unlocked the door. With a soft groan he took the action from sweet to scorching, his tongue doing things that shredded every last one of her good intentions.

Cupping the back of his head in both hands, she buried her fingers in his luxurious dark hair and slackened her jaw, allowing all the access he needed to drive her insane. She did her best to return the favor.

The prickle of his upper lip was just enough to add erotic undertones. His breathing picked up and he pulled her closer, much closer.

No mistaking that move. He wasn't shy about letting her know what he was thinking. So was she, now that he'd worked her into a lather with the most arousing first kiss of her life. If this was a prelude, she couldn't wait for the main attraction.

Now what? They could have a creative make out session in the woods, but she didn't want that. She wasn't a teenager anymore and he certainly wasn't. She was hip-to-hip with an experienced man who wouldn't be satisfied with half measures.

That said, she'd already started unbuttoning his shirt. She longed to touch his skin, feel his heart pounding and his chest heave.

He lifted his mouth a fraction away from hers. "I want you, Sara."

"Ditto, Kieran."

"Not here."

"No."

"But where?"

She swallowed. "I don't know."

"Where do you sleep?"

"In one of the kids' old rooms."

"Alone?"

"With Lani."

"Damn." Slowly, reluctantly, he loosened his grip. "Where will Desiree put me?"

"In one of those rooms. My folks are in one, too."

"Cozy."

That made her giggle. "We're a pair, aren't we?"

"That we are. I need to back away now or I'll start kissing you again, which will only make us both more frustrated." He released her and put on his hat.

"I love how you say *froostrated.*"

"I love how you look all rosy and kissed."

She pressed her hand to her hot cheeks. "I get like that. I didn't end up with freckles for some reason, but my skin turns pink really fast."

"All over?" His blue eyes sparkled with a combination of laughter and lust.

"That's a very intimate question, Mr. Haggerty."

"I meant for it to be, Miss Armstrong."

"I'd love for you to see for yourself, but I have no idea how we can ever make it happen." She took a deep breath. "And even if we manage to enjoy ourselves this week...."

"It's all we'll ever have."

"Except if I come to Dublin for work."

"But you'll be working. Not much time for other things."

"Sad but true. Will you come back here?"

"It's a lot of money."

"And I'd have to coordinate my visit with yours."

The gleam faded from his eyes. "I've told myself all that. Turns out when the chips were down, I didn't care. I had to find out what your mouth felt like."

"And?"

"Just as I thought." He gave her a crooked smile. "The lips of an angel, the tongue of a devil."

She laughed. "You're a bad, bad boy." He hadn't buttoned his shirt. She'd opened it almost to the waistband of his jeans, so she had a nice peek at his broad chest sprinkled lightly with dark hair.

"I'm as bad as they come. I shouldn't be thinking of taking you to bed. I should concentrate on the meeting with my brother. He'll soon be facing the same shock I just had."

"We should give up on this idea."

He held her gaze. "We should."

No telling how long they would have stood there enmeshed in their mutual longing if Sam hadn't bounded out of the woods, his ruff loaded with leaves and pine needles.

"Aw, Sam." Kieran started buttoning his shirt. "See what you've done. We can't be taking you home looking like that, now, can we?"

"We won't. But we need to start back so we have time to clean him up."

"Then off we go." He held out his hand.

Such a simple gesture, and so tender. Sliding her fingers through his made her chest swell with happiness.

As they started off, he gave her hand a squeeze. "I had the urge to do this on the way out. Tossed it aside."

"Feels nice."

"Yes, ma'am."

"Oh, geez. You've got me hooked, okay? That *yes, ma'am* routine is overkill."

"No such thing. When we get back, Lani will take you aside like she did earlier. She's your big sister. She has influence. I need to, um, solidify my position, if you know what I mean."

"I get it, silly man. You're ridiculous."

"Seems I'd rather tease you than think about what's coming up."

She should have figured that out. "Tease me all you want, then."

"I'd rather kiss you."

"We don't have time for that. We need to make Sam presentable."

He looked down at the collie, who'd decided to stick with the humans for the trip back. "He's a mess. Too bad we don't have a dog brush."

"We'll stop by the barn and use a curry comb on him."

"The barn?" Kieran's eyebrows rose. "There's an idea. In the dead of night, we can—"

"I'd never get past Lani."

"Then I guess you have to let her in on it."

"She doesn't approve of us getting together."

"Neither do I. It's pure foolishness to risk our hearts like that. Then again, they're ours to risk."

She let that sink in as they continued down the path. "I'll take a wild guess that's the philosophy that got you over here."

"I suppose it is. I was risking Granny's heart, too, and I asked her forgiveness in advance. I'll ask yours, as well, if we find a way to be together this week. It'll be complicated, since I need to make time to be with my brother. Assuming he wants that."

"Oh, he will."

"But he's married, and a newlywed at that. Some of his hours are spoken for."

"So are some of mine. We have the birthday party for Lani and Dallas on Saturday night. And if I know Desiree, she'll want to invite everyone over tomorrow night to meet you."

"Everybody? Like twenty people?"

"More than twenty. There's all the kids, plus my brother Trent and his wife Brittany, and now Brittany's mom is included in gatherings. The dads who've moved here might be invited, and the Wenches would be, for sure."

"The *wenches*? She invites working girls to the house?"

"It's not what you think."

"Hope not."

"Desiree started a group years ago called Wenches Who Read. It's a book club."

"A book club. Thank the Lord."

"But it's not *just* a book club."

"Sara, if they're running a brothel I don't want to hear about it."

She laughed. "They used to have a secret function, but it's not a secret anymore."

"I really don't need to know—"

"Relax. They read and critique Desiree's work before she sends it to the publisher. They also brainstorm plots and help her with story problems. Nobody in town was supposed to know Desiree's a bestselling author, so until recently they couldn't breathe a word of it."

"I was going to ask her why she decided now was the time to go public after thirty-five years."

"Gee, I wonder why you forgot?"

"I wonder."

"I think adding another bookstore has something to do with it. That's Lucky's project and she wants him to succeed. In a couple of weeks she'll do a signing at the new Louis L'Amour and More bookstore in Apple Grove. It'll be the first time M.R. Morrison has ever been seen in public."

"That should bring in business."

"Oh, yeah. My brother Trent created the marketing plan for that store. He's almost as excited about that as he is about the baby."

"When's the due date?"

"Not for six months. Brittany's not even showing yet, but Trent's already the most excited daddy-to-be I've ever seen. It's adorable."

"Do you want any?"

She glanced over to find him looking at her with an affectionate smile.

"Kids?"

"Yeah."

"Sure, someday. Why?"

"Because while you were talking about your brother's baby, I had this sudden vision of you with a round belly, and how nice you'd look."

His comment brought a flush to her cheeks and stirred a reaction deep in her core. "If you think you got a glimpse into the future, I'm not planning on it anytime soon."

"I don't know what it was. I've never looked at a woman and imagined her pregnant."

"Do *you* want kids?"

"I haven't let myself think about it. I've been too focused on this trip."

"Maybe your subconscious is telling you something."

"Could be. I haven't let myself get serious about anyone, either."

"So you put your life on hold?"

"I didn't see it that way, but yeah, that's exactly what I did."

"And now you're free to move forward, find someone special, make some babies." What a depressing image.

"Possibly."

"I hate to say it, but having a fling with me is going in the wrong direction. You need to keep your powder dry, as they say."

His brow wrinkled. "I don't get it."

"Back in the day of muskets, they used gun powder and when a big battle was coming, they had to make sure they didn't waste their powder or worse yet, let the rain get to it."

"Ah." He grinned. "No worries, lass. I've been in very few battles lately. I've kept my powder dry and I have plenty to spare."

9

Kieran hadn't been on many carnival rides in his life, mostly because they would've cut into his savings plan, but his emotions had been through some ups and downs over the years. Nothing like this, though.

He'd didn't know if he was coming or going. But he knew who he wanted in the seat beside him for the whiplash curves, steep climbs and heart-pounding drops.

If Sara could only be his companion for this week, he'd count himself blessed. If he could be allowed to hold her in his arms now and then, that would be sweeter yet. If he could make love to her, even once, he'd ask for nothing more in this life.

A curry comb made Sam presentable. While they cleaned him up, Kieran evaluated the barn as a rendezvous location. Wouldn't be his first choice, but he'd keep it in mind.

On the walk back to the house, they paused long enough to exchange phone numbers. Then he took her hand again, right before he made the mistake of asking if she had a fella back home.

She pulled her hand free. "Of course not! How could you think I had someone I cared about back home after the way I kissed you?"

"My apologies. It's just hard to imagine a woman like you doesn't have someone."

"It's hard to imagine a man like you doesn't have someone, but I gave you credit for not being a cheater."

"I'm an eejit." He snuck a glance at her rosy cheeks. Anger turned her skin pink, too. "I'm sorry, Sara. The last thing I want is to insult you. Walking into Hannigan's and finding you there was like a miracle."

That brought a tiny smile. "Did you hear a choir of angels sing?"

"I do believe I did. I even know what they were singing." He considered his next move. Why not? "Want to hear it?"

"Absolutely!"

He cleared his throat and began to sing his Granny's favorite song, the one she'd beg for whenever she was feeling down, *My Love Is Like a Red, Red Rose.*

Sara stopped in her tracks and turned to him, her lips parted in surprise and her eyes alight with fascination.

The collie turned around, too, head cocked and tail wagging slowly.

He'd captured the pair of them with a simple Irish song that was older than the hills. He'd never sung it to anyone but Granny. Grandpa had started the tradition, singing to her when Kieran was a boy. He'd learned it by osmosis.

One day he'd busted out with it when Grandpa was singing, and he'd been doing it ever since, going solo after Grandpa passed. Never thought he'd be serenading an American woman from New Jersey in front of a Montana ranch house.

Might as well do it right. Taking both her hands, he held her gaze and put his heart into it. She deserved a gift of a song after all she'd done for him. It was old-fashioned and ridiculously sentimental, but judging from the glow in her green eyes, she loved it.

When he finished, she sighed and opened her mouth to say something. Enthusiastic applause from the porch startled her into letting go of him. Then she spun around.

Made him jump, too. Evidently his rendition had carried through the open windows of the house. Three people had been added to the four who'd been there when they'd headed out for a walk — a fella he recognized as Andy, an older woman he identified as Marybeth, and another man who likely was Buck.

Everyone called out things like *great job, bravo* and *encore* to the point he felt his face heat as he and Sara approached the steps. Sara's family and Desiree stayed on the porch, but Andy, Marybeth and Buck came down to meet them.

Andy stuck out his hand. "That was beautiful, son. Never heard an Irish tenor in person before. You have a gift."

Andy's handshake was firm and his gaze steady. Clearly a fella you could count on. "My granny says so, but then she's prejudiced, isn't she?"

"She may be, but she's also right. I'm Andy Hartmann, by the way."

"Figured. Kieran Haggerty."

Andy grinned. "Figured."

"I'm Marybeth Weaver, Kieran." She put out her hand. "And this is my husband, Buck."

"Happy to meet you both." After he'd returned the handshake of the other two members of Desiree's inner circle, he understood why all three were a major part of her life. Not a plonker in the bunch.

"That was quite a performance." Marybeth flipped her long gray braid over her shoulder. "You looked gobsmacked, Sara."

"Because I was. I had no idea he could sing, let alone sound like a star. We were just joking around. I expected some goofy version of *Danny Boy*."

"That's the only Irish song I know," Buck said. "It's nice, but sad. This one's nice and nobody's dying."

"Sad songs and drinking songs." Kieran chuckled. "We love 'em."

"Do you know any drinking songs?" Marybeth gave him an assessing glance.

"I might."

"Do you know *Whiskey in the Jar*?"

"I do. There's a drinking song and a sad song rolled into one."

"How about *The Rocky Road to Dublin*?"

Buck turned to her. "Where're you coming up with these?"

"Don't forget I took that trip to Ireland the summer before we met."

"You said you went to look at castles."

"You can't look at castles at night."

"Which leaves singing and drinking in the pub, evidently."

She gave her husband a smile. Then she patted Kieran's arm. "We'll get together later and come up with a list. But now we need to head back into the house. We've had more discussion about the meeting between you and your brother and we need your input."

"All right." He glanced at Sara as they followed Andy and the Weavers up the steps. "Just so you know, I'd like you to be there."

"Are you sure? Seems like it should be just the two of you."

"It'll likely come to that after we get through the first awkward parts, but he's on his home turf, surrounded by his relations whether they're physically there or not. Granny's thousands of kilometers away and I—"

"Say no more. I'll be there."

"Thanks." He and Sara joined the procession to the living room, the same route he'd taken earlier, but oh, how his world had changed since he'd walked into the house the first time.

For one thing, Desiree urged everyone to sit down. Chairs had been added, including a striking purple wingback. He motioned Sara to a dining chair and he took the one that was next to it. The upholstered seats should go to the older adults.

Lani grabbed another of the dining chairs and Buck claimed the fourth, insisting he preferred it. The chair also put him close to Marybeth, who sat with Vanessa and Harry on the couch. Desiree claimed the purple wingback and Andy took the other easy chair after unsuccessfully trying to trade with Buck.

Desiree glanced around and finally let her gaze rest on him and Sara. "As you two probably guessed, I called Andy at the newspaper the second you two were out the door. Then I texted Marybeth and Buck."

Kieran looked at Andy. "You came from town? How long have you been here?"

"Close to thirty minutes. I might've ignored the speed limit."

"I knew he'd drive like a bat out of hell, but I decided it was daylight so he wasn't in too much danger of killing himself. And I wanted his advice, along with Marybeth and Buck's on how to approach Lucky."

"Instead of meeting him in town after the shop closes?"

"Not necessarily. But I think it might be kinder if I call now and tell him about you on the phone rather than have you show up in person when he's had no chance to prepare."

The prospect zipped through his system as if he'd touched a live wire. "Call him *now*?"

"Think about how you reacted when I told you. And he wasn't even in the room. What if he had been here at the time?"

He gulped. "No telling. God knows it would have been a holy show."

"I'm in favor of the phone call," Andy said. "Then Dez can give him the choice of where he wants this meeting to take place."

Andy's use of *Dez* surprised him. You couldn't hang a nickname on a legend... could you? "I hadn't thought it through, but it makes sense to call him. In his shoes I'd want a chance to get over the initial shock. I've had that chance. He should, too."

"And," Desiree continued, "he can decide who he wants to be there."

"And so can I."

She blinked. "You've decided that already?"

"Yes, ma'am." He didn't look at Sara when he said it. She had to be giggling inside. "As far as I'm concerned, any or all of you can be there. But I specifically want Sara. She volunteered to help me through this, and although it's not turning out anything like she expected, I'm holding her to her promise."

Her cheeks turned pink, likely because she was fighting the urge to bust out laughing. "I wouldn't miss it for the world."

"Then I guess it's settled. I'll call him now, but not here. I'll make the call from my bedroom so he can swear all he wants."

Kieran chuckled. "Wish I'd had that option."

She gazed at him. "You controlled your language?"

"I did."

"Do you normally swear a lot?"

"Compared to my mates? No. Compared to folks from over here?" He grinned. "Americans are good at many things, but swearing's not one of them."

10

In the silence that fell after Desiree left the room, Sara had a pretty good idea what her mom and Lani were focused on. She did her best not to squirm as they glanced at her.

She took a stab at conversation. "Good thing Lucky's here at least, and not in Apple Grove."

"Very good," Andy said.

Lani didn't comment. Any second now she'd ask a question about the walk. She had to be dying to know what the eff had prompted Kieran to break into song.

"Speaking of Apple Grove." Her dad looked across at Andy. "I have a taste for some of that pale ale Lucky brought back. Think we could head for the kitchen and round up some drinks and snacks for this crew?" He pushed up from the couch.

"Great idea, Harry." Andy left his chair. "Shoulda thought of it myself."

"I could go for that." Buck got up, too. "Want some, Marybeth?"

"Sure. Thanks."

"Vanessa?" Her dad quirked an eyebrow at her mom.

"Sounds good."

His gaze shifted to his daughters. "Girls?"

"I'm in." Sara looked at Kieran. "I doubt they have any Guinness."

"We don't," Andy said. "But I think we can find you something that'll work."

"I'll bet you can." He left his chair. "I'll go see what they've got and bring your ale while I'm at it. What can I get you, Lani?"

"Same. Thanks, Kieran."

Once they'd all left for the kitchen, Marybeth chuckled. "How nice of them to leave us alone for some girl talk."

"Harry could feel it coming," her mom said. "After living in a house with three women, he has a keen sense of when I'd like him to vacate the premises." She smiled as male laughter erupted from the kitchen. "Besides, it's a treat for him to commune with the guys."

"We need to talk fast, though." Lani zeroed in on Sara. "C'mon, girl, give. When a man spontaneously bursts into song in the middle of a sunny afternoon, there's gotta be a reason."

"Irishmen don't necessarily need a reason." Marybeth got a faraway look in her eyes. "They just love to sing."

Sara turned to her. "Sounds like you had a fabulous time that summer. Did you stay in one part or—"

"Nice try, Sara." Lani pinned her with a look. "But we can talk about Marybeth's trip while the men are in the room, whereas—"

"Not if you want to hear the good stuff," Marybeth said. "But you're right. Now's not the time. Sara, you're up."

"He kissed me. And I kissed him back. End of story."

Marybeth smiled. "Looks like the beginning of one to me."

"Me, too," Lani said. "The beginning of a doomed love affair. But there's still time to save yourself, sis. I'll admit he's damned attractive. It's no mystery to me why you want to jump his bones, but—"

"It's not only that. He needs a friend."

"He does." Her mom nodded. "I found it touching that he wants you there when he meets Lucky."

"I agree it's touching, Mom." Lani was clearly intent on making her case. "But he'll have that meeting in the next few hours. Mission accomplished. After that, she can back away so she won't be miserable when they each go their separate ways in a week."

Her mom's gaze was tender as she turned in her direction. "It's not a bad idea, Sara. He'll be bonding with his brother, with all the McLintocks. He'll be surrounded by a family he never knew he had."

"If I wanted to pull away, that would be the perfect time. The thing is, I don't want to."

"Because he's beautiful, sweetie." Marybeth reached over from the couch and squeezed her knee. "We all understand that."

"We just don't want you to get hurt," her mom said. "Or Kieran, either. I like him. If he didn't live in Ireland, I'd be dancing a jig over this situation."

"Would he consider living in the US?" Lani glanced at Sara. "If that's a possibility...."

"Not as long as his granny's alive. She's firmly planted in their little village and he'd never leave her." She took a breath. "I hear what you're saying and I know you're both looking out for me. So is he. This afternoon he admitted that getting involved and risking our hearts is foolish."

"There, see?" Lani smiled. "He gets it."

"He also said they're ours to risk."

Marybeth sighed. "Spoken like a true Irishman. They're so passion—"

"Fair warning, ladies," her father called out. "If you're saying anything you don't want us to hear, better lock it down. The men are on the move."

Her mom flashed her a grin. "He's lovin' this."

"Lucky's on his way!" Desiree sailed out of the bedroom, cheeks flushed.

"He is?" Andy set a tray loaded with frosty bottles on the large coffee table. "He's already adjusted to the news?"

"Hell, no. He was shocked to his toes. Dropped the phone. He says the screen's cracked but it still works. He was in the storeroom with the door closed, so at least the customers didn't see him in berserker mode."

Andy frowned. "Is he safe to drive?"

"If he's not, Oksana will insist on driving them here. At one point he said he'd need time to wrap his head around it. But after we talked and talked and talked some more, he said he'd close up early and come home. And he's bringing Rance."

"*What?*" Andy's eyes widened. "Why?"

"It's the right thing to do," Marybeth said. "I've been thinking about Rance this whole time. He and Lucky grew up as twins. This'll rock his world, too."

"Sure, but—"

"I agree with Marybeth," Desiree's breathless delivery betrayed her agitation. "Rance is about an hour into his shift at the Buffalo. He rode in with Clint so Lucky and Oksana are stopping by there to pick him up. Somehow they'll convince Clint to give him time off without saying why."

Sara glanced at Kieran, who looked like he might be having a panic attack of his own. He'd hooked two bottles of pale ale between the fingers of one hand, a precarious setup since he was freaking out. In his other hand, he white-knuckled a can of beer. He'd already put a dent in it.

"Lani," she said in a low voice. "Take those bottles from him."

"Got it."

He glanced down as Lani slipped the bottles away. "Thanks."

"Thank you for bringing them." She spoke to him in her big sister voice.

Sara wrapped both hands around his closed fist and the dented beer can. "I doubt you could actually crush it, but you could make a mess."

"Huh?" He looked at the beer can as if he'd never seen it before. "Oh." Loosening his grip, he examined the dent. "Yeah, that's not good. Don't know what I was thinking."

"Want me to take it?"

He nodded. "Might choke on it."

"He'll be as nervous as you are," Desiree said.

"I'm not nervous."

"It's okay to be—"

"I'm terrified. What am I going to say? What if we have no bleedin' idea how to talk to each other and we just sit there in silence?"

"You won't." Desiree met his gaze. "I promise."

"How do you know?"

"Rance. No one sits in awkward silence when he's around."

That brought a rueful laugh from Lani. "That's for sure. Sometimes you just want to—" She caught herself and shrugged. "He'll keep things going."

"He will." Desiree's tense shoulders dropped slightly. "Lucky's instincts were on target." She accepted the frosty bottle Andy handed her. "Thanks, my love." Taking a sip, she looked around the room. "Now we need to consider the venue."

"If it'll be this room, it's my opinion we should all clear out except for Sara." Andy checked Desiree's reaction.

"Yeah, they don't need a cast of thousands hanging around."

"We can move the party to Rowdy Roost," her dad said. "That's easy enough."

"Or…" Desiree looked at Kieran. "You could have your meetup in there."

"In where? What's Rowdy Roost?"

"A game room."

"A game room on steroids." Sara's anxiety level lowered a bit. "I think that's brilliant. If they run out of things to say they can play darts."

"Darts?" A spark of interest chased some of the worry from Kieran's eyes.

Marybeth clapped a hand to her forehead. "I can't believe I didn't think of that." She gazed up at him. "I assume you play."

A faint smile lifted the corners of his mouth. "I've been known to, yeah."

"Translated, he's amazing at it. Watch out for sandbagging."

"Hey, Sara." Desiree motioned to her. "Let's take Kieran to Rowdy Roost and see if he thinks it'll work."

"I think he'll like it."

"If it has a dart board, that's a good start." He glanced toward the dog bed where Sam lay, head up and ears pricked. "Sam looks like he'd like to come along."

"By all means. Okay, Sam." Desiree patted her thigh. "You're invited, too." She glanced up at Kieran. "He's taken a shine to you."

"The feeling's mutual. Looks like he knows where he's going."

"Sam likes Rowdy Roost. Reminds him of all the parties there, which are his favorites. He'll be a good icebreaker for this meeting." Desiree followed the collie through the dining room.

"Dogs are good for that." Kieran waited for Sara to start after Desiree and then he fell in step beside her. His hand brushed hers and he linked their pinky fingers.

Cute. She glanced over and smiled.

"I know this first day will be kinda tough for you and Lucky," Desiree said, "but in the end, what a gift you'll be to each other."

"I've thought of that. This has already been the most important day of my life. And it's not even over." He looked over at her.

She caught her breath. Maybe he was only thinking of her role in getting him to Desiree. But the warmth in his gaze sent a far more intimate message.

11

When Desiree flipped a switch, old-fashioned lanterns with red shades lit up a space that looked more like a film set than a family game room. An antique wooden bar only slightly smaller than the one at the Buffalo stretched across the wall to Kieran's left. On his right, stairs led to a narrow balcony across a wall painted to look as if a second story contained hotel rooms.

Round wooden tables and chairs scattered around the room were the type where gamblers in fancy vests might hang out, luring in local cowboys to bet their week's pay. The room was big enough to accommodate a full-sized pool table with a shamrock green felt surface.

He'd played on smaller tables in his favorite pub back home. He wouldn't hold his own against Lucky or any of the McLintocks if this was the setup where they honed their skills.

The dartboard, though, held promise. He'd spent many nights, probably too many, at that game. His mates were good, but he was better. Competing with a fella at darts was a good way to assess his character. Might come in handy this afternoon.

Desiree swept a hand around the room. "Think this'll work?"

"It's a grand place you have here. Never seen anything like it except Miss Kitty's saloon in *Gunsmoke*."

Desiree's eyebrows lifted. "That's a great compliment."

He glanced at Sara. "I don't suppose you watched that."

She shook her head. "But the more time I spend here, the more I want to catch up on those old shows. This ranch is great. To think I was scared to come for a visit."

That surprised him. "You? Scared?"

"I'm a city girl. Growing up I lived in a neighborhood where the houses were close together and the wildlife consisted of birds and the occasional squirrel."

"To be honest, that's mostly what I see in our wee village, too. But for some reason I'm not scared of the wildlife here."

"You probably don't have sadistic friends like mine. They've kept me supplied with a stream of news reports about someone mauled by a grizzly, trampled by a moose, bitten by a rattler, eaten by a mountain lion." She ticked off the options on her fingers.

"The same person?"

She grinned. "Different people. For one person that would add up to a really bad day."

"Wow." Desiree's eyes twinkled. "What a terrifying list. I'm surprised you got on that plane back in February."

"By that time I'd figured out my friends were afraid I'd fall in love with the place and move here like my two brothers did. I have fallen in love with it but they didn't have to worry. I'm not planning to leave them or my awesome job."

He didn't want her to leave her job, either. It was his only hope for seeing her again, assuming she made it to Dublin as she'd predicted. Or London. He'd meet her there if it came to that. Even Paris wasn't out of the question.

Bottom line, he would see her again. Somehow. The idea that she'd disappear from his life was unacceptable.

"Neither of you brought your drinks when we came out here. Do you want me to go get them?"

He shook his head. "I thought it would settle my nerves, but I don't want to be sitting here enjoying a beer when they come in."

"Why not?"

"It seems... disrespectful. Lucky closed up shop early so he could make this meeting happen sooner. He and his wife... what did you say her name was?"

"Oksana."

"Lucky and Oksana likely had things to do, but they dropped everything for me. Rance will be missing work, too. What does he do there?"

"Mostly bartending. Sometimes serving if he's needed."

"Which means they'll be a man down behind the bar because of me. Greeting them with a beer in my hand isn't right. Granny wouldn't approve, I can tell you that."

"Well, if you all decide to have something after they arrive, the fridge behind the bar is stocked."

"Thanks. That's a better plan."

"Speaking of your granny, have you found a moment to contact her? I'll bet she'll be blown away."

"That she will, but it's the middle of the night. I'd give her a heart attack."

"Oh, *right*. It's good you remembered that. When Andy and I were in Kenya I got a call in the middle of the night. Totally freaked me out."

"Kenya?"

"For our honeymoon. I'll show you pictures later. Anyway, an editorial assistant who didn't know I was out of the country called about a minor...." Her breath caught as Sam trotted to the wide double door on the far side of the room. "They're here."

He gulped. "You're staying, yeah?"

"No. I might try to direct things." She hugged him and then Sara. "You'll be fine." Turning, she left quickly, pushing through the swinging louvered doors into the hallway.

His gut churning, he turned to Sara. "This is it."

"It'll be awesome."

"Thanks for being here." Leaning down, he gave her a quick kiss. "For luck." The response that flared in her eyes was a welcome distraction from the heavy thud of his heart. He promised himself they'd enjoy a longer kiss the first chance they had.

Truck doors opened and closed. A woman's calm voice mingled with the deeper, more agitated tones of two fellas. Then one of them sang the first few words of *Danny Boy.* Not bad, either. The other shushed him.

Kieran pegged Rance as the singer and Lucky as the one who'd cut him off. Taking a breath was torture when his lungs felt like they were made of steel, but he forced himself to do it so he wouldn't be light-headed when they came in.

And why in God's name was he just standing still like a buck eejit? Striding toward the door, he grabbed the handle of the right-hand door and yanked it open.

The three people on the other side jumped back with a yell of surprise.

Lucky. Recognition was instantaneous, a knowing that sank into his chest and seeped through his pores. *My brother.* The clues were there — the hair, the chin, the body build, a long-ago memory of those green eyes.

But he didn't need any of it. Had he felt this connection all along? Had some primitive link driven him to live like a pauper until he'd saved enough to cross the ocean?

Lucky stared at him with the same fascination, the same wonder that kept Kieran glued to the spot, afraid to move in case he was dreaming.

Then the other fella—Rance—doubled over laughing.

Kieran snapped out of his daze. "Sorry!" Heat rose to his face. "I just decided—"

"To scare the crap out of us?" Rance choked out, taking off his hat and wiping his eyes on his sleeve. "Mission accomplished."

"Don't mind Rance." Lucky's intense gaze remained locked with his. "He's easily amused." Then he held out his hand and his voice roughened. "It's like… it's like I know you."

When his fingers closed around Lucky's hand, his throat closed and pressure built behind his eyes. He blinked away tears and managed a response. "Same here."

Lucky's grip tightened and he swallowed. "I guess because…" He cleared his throat. "You look like… me."

12

Sara pulled a tissue out of her jeans pocket and quietly dabbed at her eyes. A glance at Oksana caught her doing the same.

Even Rance stood in subdued silence as Lucky and Kieran held their position, hands clasped, emotions bubbling below the surface. Sam parked himself to one side, his attention darting from one to the other.

Then Kieran's shoulders slowly relaxed and the corners of his mouth tilted ever so slightly. "Fancy a hug?"

Laughter flashed in Lucky's eyes. "Sure. What the hell."

They embraced, held on for a second and then stepped away from each other, grinning. Sam pranced around them, tail wagging in approval.

"How about me?" Rance said. "Don't I get a hug? I've been watching out for this guy, keeping him out of trouble while I waited all these years for you to get here."

"Then I owe you." Kieran gave Rance an enthusiastic hug.

"Oh, you definitely owe me." Rance's eyes sparkled with mischief. "He tested my patience many times, but somebody had to be the adult in the room."

Sara laughed. "That's not how I heard it. More like the other way around. Wasn't Lucky the one constantly saving your ass?"

"Well, now that you mention it, I do recall—"

"Whether I have or haven't," Lucky said. "You came through back in February, and that totally evened the score. Without you, I wouldn't be with this wonderful woman." Reaching for Oksana's hand, he drew her up beside him. "Oksana, meet my brother Kieran."

She smiled and shook his hand. "What a special day. You two do look a lot alike."

"Yes, ma'am."

"*Yes, ma'am*? Lucky, he even sounds like you!"

"You can thank Sara for that." He gave her a quick glance. "She taught me that it was common around here. Where I'm from, it's not."

"Sara taught you, did she?" Rance gave her a wink. "Rumor has it there's more than language lessons going on between you two."

Her cheeks warmed. "I just happened to be buying a hat when he came into Hannigan's looking for the same thing."

"Classic cute meet. He wants your hat and is willing to wrestle you for it. After twenty minutes of rolling around on the floor of Hannigan's, you fall madly in love and decide to share custody of the hat."

Kieran chuckled "Well done. I couldn'ta described it better. I'm thinking you have Irish blood, yeah?"

"Sadly, I'm British on both sides."

Sara latched onto that tidbit. Rance had never mentioned his father. Every other McLintock child knew their father's name and had a story to go with it. She'd been hesitant to ask about his.

"British, is it?" Kieran shook his head. "That's a bleedin' shame. You should dig a little deeper, uncover that Irish ancestor."

"I'll do it for you, buddy. In the meantime, who's up for a libation? This party could use a little grease on the wheels, if you get my drift." He walked behind the bar, pulled out a large bag of popcorn and filled two bowls. "What'll it be, ladies and gents?"

"The darkest beer you've got," Kieran moved over to take a stool at the bar and everyone else followed suit.

Kieran and Lucky ended up together in the middle with the women on either side. Sara didn't think it was an accident. The two men had stayed close to each other ever since Lucky had come through the door.

"Pale ale for me." Lucky looked at Oksana, who nodded. "Make that two."

"Three." Sara hoped somebody was drinking the one she'd left in the living room, but she wasn't going back after it and risk missing something.

"Let me see what's here." Rance opened the mini-fridge behind the bar. "Looks like plenty of ale. Here's a dark lager that might work for you,

Kieran." He uncapped the bottle and passed it over, along with a coaster.

"It will. Thanks."

"If I'd known the situation, I would've brought some Guinness from town. Certain people kept the details from me until I was in the truck."

"I couldn't tell you in front of Clint. It was hard enough convincing him nobody was hurt or dead."

"And you promised to let Clint know the reason ASAP." Rance passed out the chilled bottles of ale and more coasters before uncapping one for himself. "ASAP has come and gone."

"Oh, well. He'll hear about it eventually." Lucky gazed at his half-brother. "Making this trip took guts. Here's to you." He raised his bottle.

"To Kieran!" everyone called out.

Color rose to his cheeks as he touched his bottle to each of theirs. "And to all of you for taking me in."

"Except we're just a few of the many." Sara helped herself to popcorn from the bowl closest to her and then nudged it toward Kieran. "When will the rest find out?"

"Mom told me on the phone that she'd like to give Kieran and me a chance to talk before she brings in the whole gang. And I'm loaded with questions."

Kieran swallowed a mouthful of beer. "Let's hear 'em."

"For starters, Mom said we have a grandmother back in County Kildare."

"That we do." He pulled out his phone. "She hates me taking her picture, but she let me take one when she was dressed up for Easter Sunday." He gave Sara a quick peek before handing the phone to Lucky.

He chuckled. "Love the hat."

"She's convinced the more flowers on her hat, the better God likes it."

"I'm sure that's true." Lucky studied the picture, his expression softening. "She's blonde?"

"From a bottle. There's plenty of older pictures at the house of her, her and Grandpa."

"He's gone, though?"

"Ten years ago. You woulda liked him."

Lucky took a ragged breath. "Yeah."

"She was a beauty like mum. Long black hair, green eyes."

"She's still a beauty." Lucky's voice was husky. "Have you told her?" He handed back the phone.

"Like I said to Desiree, it's the middle of the night. They're seven hours ahead."

"Sure. Right." He nodded. "We had to figure that out when Mom and Andy went to Kenya. When were you going to contact her?"

"Haven't decided the best time. Wanna be there?"

"I do. With Oksana." He looked over at her. "You want to, right?"

"You know I do, but... I think it's better if it's just you and Kieran. Let her get over the shock and surprise. I can be in on another call."

Lucky glanced at Kieran. "What do you think?"

"She's right. I think its best if you and I are the only ones this first time."

"All right."

"Fancy a game of darts while we figure out a time to call?"

Lucky gave him an assessing glance. "Yes, I believe I do."

Kieran turned to her. "Wanna play, Sara?"

She smiled. "You're sweet to ask, but unless Oksana—"

"Not me. I'll take Lucky on in a chess game any day, but almost nobody can touch him at darts."

"Yeah?" Kieran glanced at him, anticipation in his voice. "Pretty good, are you?"

"Decent."

Rance snorted. "Uh-huh. Like Michael Jordan was a *decent* basketball player."

"Should be an interesting game, then." Kieran picked up his lager and slid off the stool.

Sara watched them saunter toward the dart board, Sam trotting behind them, as they discussed something to do with the type of dartboard. "They have the same walk."

"They do." Oksana moved over to Kieran's stool. "Aren't you loving this?"

"It's fabulous. For both of them. What do you think, Rance?"

"Tell you in a sec. I'm adding atmosphere to this shindig." He fiddled with something behind the bar. "Ah, there we go." A rollicking tune poured from the Rowdy Roost's wall-mounted speakers.

Was that an Irish drinking song? Catchy. She tapped her toe against the bar's foot rail.

Kieran turned around and looked at Rance. "Don't tell me you had *The Rocky Road to Dublin* lying around."

"No, sir. I found an Irish playlist on our streaming service."

His eyebrows rose. "Savage."

"You don't like it?"

"I like it a lot."

"*Savage* equals approval?"

"It does."

"Okay, then." He gave Kieran a thumbs up, then quickly slapped his hand down on the bar. "If that was an insult, you never saw it."

"Not an insult, Yank." Kieran grinned and returned the gesture before turning away.

"Yank?" Rance muttered. "Are we in a World War II movie?"

"That's what they label all of us." Sara grabbed another handful of popcorn. "I led a four-day New York City tour for a bunch of people from Dublin. It was quite an education."

"That puts you ahead of the rest of us," Oksana said.

"Not by much. So Rance, what do you think of Kieran? Devious move, by the way, putting on music so he can't hear us talk about him."

"You wound me, dear lady."

"Come on, Rance," Oksana said. "We know your tricks. Tell us what you think."

"I'll cut to the chase. Kieran needs to switch countries." He gave Sara a meaningful glance before returning his attention to Oksana. "And bring his cute-as-hell granny. I doubt he'd up and leave her there and we're low on grandmas, anyway."

"Desiree's a grandma." Oksana took a sip of her ale.

"Yeah, but she doesn't look like one. That Irish lady does. I'll bet she bakes cookies and lets you lick the spoon."

"They're called biscuits over there." Sara had learned that from the Dublin group, but her mind wasn't on cookies. Why had Rance immediately suggested that Kieran relocate? And what was with the piercing look he'd given her?

"Biscuits, cookies, whatever. She's the type who bakes them. It would be like having a second Marybeth, only she'd have an Irish accent and be spouting all those funny Irish sayings."

Time to put a stop to that daydream. "It won't be happening. According to Kieran, his sweet-looking granny's never traveled except on her honeymoon and that wasn't far from home. There's virtually no chance she'd leave Ireland."

"Yeah, well, what does he know?"

"A lot, considering he's her only close relative."

"Which means he should have plenty of influence when push comes to shove. Wouldn't you like it if he decided to live in the good ol' US of A, Miss Sara?"

"If you're trying to matchmake, forget it. Too many moving parts."

"Some more important than others." He waggled his eyebrows.

Oksana grinned. "Don't tease her. She just met the guy a few hours ago."

"That's what's impressive. They just met, but if you didn't know that, you'd think they'd been together for weeks. Maybe months. That's a situation that should be nurtured."

Sara gazed at him. "I appreciate the thought, but it's a non-starter."

"Are you sure about that? Because after only ten minutes of watching you two I was thinking you'd found the one." He turned to Oksana. "Am I wrong?"

"I could see it, too."

"Look, you guys, I'm not quitting my fabulous job to move here. Kieran has built a life in Ireland and his granny, who's gotta be around eighty, has never set foot outside of the country. I don't see a happily-ever-after in this scenario."

Rance threw up his hands. "My mistake. Guess I'm imagining things."

"No, you're not. I'm attracted to him."

"Then what are you gonna do about it?"

She sighed. "I don't know. It's complicated."

"If you want my help, let me know."

"What does that mean?"

"It's not as complicated as you're making it, but you will need help. I'm offering."

"I'll think about it."

Oksana nodded. "You should."

Sara's attention slid past Oksana to the dart game on the far side of the room and the broad-shouldered man standing there, his muscular arm cocked. Snapping it forward, he hit the exact center of the bullseye.

When Lucky groaned and hung his head, Kieran slung an arm around his shoulders and muttered something that made Lucky grin. The next moment they were laughing and toasting each other.

This Irishman had shown up and turned everyone's world upside down, including hers. She wanted him, and he'd already admitted he felt the same about her. Rance had offered his help.

Was she a fool to risk it? Or a fool if she let the opportunity pass her by?

_13_

Kieran had met his match. Lucky was the best bleedin' player he'd ever come up against. On the flip side of the coin, Lucky wasn't having an easy time of it, either.

He didn't whine though, and his cursing was mild compared to what flew around in the village pub. Not surprising. After all, he'd been raised in America. Kieran sensed a talent for it in the fire Lucky kept hidden.

He had the same fire. Granny said it came from his mother, so he'd kept it mostly hidden, too. Before he left Wagon Train, he'd talk to Lucky, tell him he wasn't alone. And the fire was a gift.

In short breaks between games, they quenched their thirst, gave Sam some pets and talked about the easy stuff like work and play — his construction and Lucky's bookshop business, what they did in their spare time. He told Lucky about Bailey and found out Lucky's horse was Silver, the white one he'd seen on the walk with Sara.

As if by an unspoken agreement, they didn't discuss their mum. He thought about her, though. Figured Lucky was thinking about her, too. Was she looking down on them, her heart filled with joy that they'd found each other? He wasn't sure he believed that, but it was a touching thought.

When yet another game ended in a tie, he gazed at his brother. *His brother.* He never would have believed those words could exist in his world. "I don't think I can beat ya, mate."

Lucky smiled. "Oh, I think you can once you've rested up. Halfway through the first game I remembered you were jet-lagged. And still giving me a tough time." He raised his hand, palm out. "Let's call it."

Kieran gripped his hand and squeezed. "Done."

"And we'll talk to Granny at nine in the morning, right?" He returned his darts to the caddy hanging on the wall.

Kieran followed suit. "As long as Oksana can do without you in the shop."

"It's scary how well she can do without me in that shop."

"Then nine it is. That's when Granny will be having afternoon tea. And after we hang up, she'll have plenty of time before it gets dark to run round to the neighbors, spreading the news."

Lucky picked up their empty bottles from a nearby table. "And there's absolutely no chance she'll turn on her video?"

"I'd bet my life on it. She refused to learn. When I showed her how it works and she saw her face on my phone, she yelled and ran out of the room. She almost gave up on the phone altogether."

"Did you tell her nobody looks good on a video chat?"

"I did, and she said *what the feck good is it, then*? Which tells you how upset she was. She's not one for swearing."

Lucky grinned. "Mom doesn't like video chats, either. I want her to do some for M.R. Morrison fans who can't make it to an in-person signing. She's dragging her feet."

"Why? She looks grand."

"I think so, but she's not happy with her resting face."

"Her what?"

"Her expression when she's just sitting there listening, not smiling or talking."

"Ah. That's what Granny's objecting to, her resting face. I didn't know what to call it."

"I understand her feeling awkward. I just wish I could see...."

"You'd like to see her face, resting or not. That's natural. But she—"

"Would she come over here? Make the trip next time you come? I'd pay for her flight. And yours."

"That would be a lot of money, mate."

"But worth it to me."

The longing in his brother's eyes made his chest tighten. He couldn't even say when he'd be coming back, let alone promise to bring Granny. Money was a problem, and he wasn't taking handouts.

But with his granny, it was more than money blocking the way. "I wish I could say she'd come, but she's never been on a plane, let alone one crossing the ocean. I don't think there's much chance."

"Then Oksana and I will have to fly over there."

"Doesn't seem like you have the time. Running two shops and all."

"We'll make the time. Last February I was at peace with the idea of never having blood relatives. But now I have you and her and it's… it's a big deal."

"For me, too. All this time I had a brother. If I'd come sooner— "

"You didn't know. It could have been a wild goose chase. And we have a lot of years ahead of us, but Granny… she must be getting up there."

"She's eighty-one."

"In good health?"

He shrugged. "A few aches and pains. Nothing serious, yeah?"

"I missed meeting our grandpa. I don't want to miss her."

"She won't want to miss you, either. But I just don't see her getting on a plane."

"Not even to visit the cemetery?"

His breath hitched. He'd pushed the gravesite to the back of his mind. He wanted to go, but it would be… challenging.

The prospect of laying flowers on her daughter's grave might convince Granny to come to Montana, though. "That could possibly work, but… don't count on it."

"If I know Mom, she's already found someone to put the right name on the stone. She knew Jane Smith couldn't be right but she had to put something on it."

"Course she did."

"I keep saying it in my head. Freya Noreen Haggerty. Can you imagine how much it means to know that name?"

"Yeah, I can." And here they were at last, talking about their fiery mother. "It's a good name. Freya means noble lady and Noreen means honor."

"That's…. kind of sad."

"She didn't live up to it." He sighed. "Granny claims she spoiled her, blames herself for her headstrong ways."

"Maybe she was headstrong. She certainly had terrible taste in men. But Mom said she was determined to pull herself out of the nosedive, take back her life and be a good mother."

"Then let's focus on that."

"Yeah, let's focus on that." Lucky took a deep breath. "Ready for me to contact Mom?"

"Desiree?" Even though he didn't think Lucky was proposing a séance, he felt the need to ask.

His brother gave him a lopsided smile. "I've never had to clarify that before. I meant Desiree. She's the only one I call Mom. Her face is the one that comes up when I use that word."

"I wish I could remember our mum's face."

"But you have the picture. And probably more at home."

"Some, but when I look at a picture, she seems like a stranger."

"What do you remember?"

"Wee bits and pieces. Sleepy eyes. A scrap of a lullaby. Pulling on her hair. Not much. I had a toy train made of wood. It's still up in Granny's attic. That train makes me think of her. We must have played with it together."

"Why didn't she bring you to America?"

"She wanted to. Granny put her foot down."

"If she had, we could have been adopted together."

"Maybe." Or he might not have made it that far. No point in saying so. "Anyway, let's contact your mum. It's time."

"Fair warning, once we leave this room, the floodgates will open. This family is huge and getting bigger every day. It could be overwhelming."

"I've always envied the ones with big families. Seemed like the craic was always better when you had more relations around."

"Crack?" Lucky's eyes widened. "Drugs?"

"Craic." He spelled it out. "It's our word for fun."

"Whew, that's a relief. I wouldn't throw that word around unless you have a chance to explain it. Folks will think it's something completely different."

"Thanks for the warning."

"So you're okay with getting inundated with relatives?"

"That I am. It'll be savage." As long as he had Sara by his side, he'd be fine. As he crossed the room, she turned, her gaze meeting his. The welcome shining in her green eyes lifted his heart and made his stomach flutter. He wanted to touch her, hold her, but he had no excuse, unless....

Until this moment, the music on the sound system had provided a comforting touch of home but he hadn't paid much attention to any of the tunes after commenting on *The Rocky Road to Dublin.*

But it just so happened the one playing now was a favorite. He'd danced to it many a time on the worn floor of the neighborhood pub. When he reached Sara, he held out his hand. "Dance with me?"

She laughed. "Sure, why not?"

He spun her into his arms and held on tight. It was the only way she'd be able to follow the crazy mashup of waltz and Irish jig footwork he and his mates had created as young bucks.

She stumbled at first but then she caught his rhythm. And they were off, whirling around the room and stomping their feet while their audience of three clapped along and Sam pranced on the outskirts, tail wagging.

"What's this song?"

"*Galway Girl.*" He relished the feel of her body making constant contact with his. Her warmth called to him, making him long for soft sheets and silky skin. His hidden fire smoldered, the embers heating, fanned to life by the music and the woman in his arms.

The fella in the song surrendered to his fiery need for a girl he'd just met and the poor soul lost his heart along the way. A high price, yeah, but when he looked into Sara's green eyes, he was more than willing to pay it.

<u>14</u>

The sexual energy Kieran brought to the dance left Sara flushed and breathless. If he brought this much passion to a simple dance, then what was she waiting for?

She gulped for air as the song ended. Whatever Rance had in mind, she was ready to hear it. Too bad she hadn't come to that conclusion earlier, but it had taken this dance to put her over the top.

As their audience whooped and hollered their approval of the fancy footwork, Kieran let her go with obvious reluctance. "Thanks for putting up with that. Probably not your usual style."

"It was fun." She almost added *and it turned me on*, but honesty wasn't the best policy while three very interested people were in the room waiting to see what happened next.

For sure it wouldn't be what she longed for. Lucky and Oksana exchanged a look of amusement as she walked back to the bar. Rance lifted a hand to his ear, pinky finger and thumb extended in the *call me* gesture.

"I've talked to Mom," Lucky announced. "Told her we're headed back to the living room.

Turns out Sky is there. He came up to the house looking for Buck, saw that I was parked by the side entrance to the Roost, and Mom had to tell him what was going on."

Rance turned off the music and rinsed out the empty popcorn bowls. "That makes three out of ten who know and one more, Clint, who's damned suspicious."

"Don't forget Trent."

"Trent, the Wenches, maybe even the dads. The word needs to go out pronto, before anybody else shows up."

Lucky nodded. "I agree. Let's go." He and Oksana led the way out through the swinging bar doors.

Rance motioned Sara and Kieran ahead of him and he brought up the rear.

Kieran glanced at her. "Tell me something about Sky."

"Rance can do a better job than I can."

"He's the oldest." Rance lowered his voice. "And the wisest, but don't tell him I said so. You can't get mad at the guy because he's so blasted reasonable. He and Buck are in charge of the barn and the horses. Sky took on that job when he was a teenager and it's been his ever since."

Kieran nodded. "Sounds like a fella I'll like."

"I like them all." Sara looked back at Rance and grinned. "Even you."

"*Even* me? What the hell does that mean?"

"Have you forgotten the wedding reception? You didn't make the best first impression."

"Ancient history."

Kieran glanced over his shoulder as they followed Lucky and Oksana down the hall. "Were you an eejit, mate?"

"I was a lot younger then."

Sara rolled her eyes. "It was six months ago."

"What'd he do?"

"Lani and I got mad because he'd ask me to dance, then Lani, then me again, then Lani like he was trying to decide which one to go after."

"It was a hard choice!"

Kieran laughed. "And they gave you the boot, yeah?"

"More or less. They sat me down and informed me we could never be more than friends because they were both staying in Trenton. End of story."

"Sounds like they did you a kindness."

"They did, and as I told Sara a little while ago, I'm ready to return that kindness."

"Oh?"

"She can tell you about it. Not now, but later."

Sara lowered her voice. "Tell him what? You weren't specific."

"You didn't ask for details."

"You have some?"

"Of course. I don't make vague promises."

She blew out a breath. If only she'd asked for details. She should have guessed his creative brain would have come up with a plan. But she hadn't been willing to commit.

When they reached the living room, Sky came straight over, hand extended. "I'm *so* glad to meet you." His gaze shifted to Lucky. "Big day, bro."

"No kidding. Listen, Rance and I think it's time to tell everybody. Kieran says he's looking forward to it."

"That I am." He added his nod of assent. "The sooner the better."

"Mom was just talking about that," Sky said.

"Then we're on the same page." Lucky raised his voice. "Mom, do you want to send a group text or—"

"You do it for the family, Lucky. It's your news. I'll handle texting the Wenches."

"Okay." He took out his phone and quickly added Trent to his list of siblings. "What should I say?" He turned toward Rance. "What's the best way to put it?"

"Short and sweet. *Dinner at the house tonight. My half-brother from—*"

"Hang on. Are we having dinner here? Mom, do you want—"

"Yes. But tell them to bring something."

Rance pointed to the screen. "Then say *Dinner at the house tonight. Bring food. My half-brother from Ireland showed up.*"

Lucky typed quickly and studied the message. "That's it? Seems abrupt."

"Trust me, it's all you need. It'll set off a stampede. They'll get the rest of the story when they arrive."

"Buck and I need to bring in the horses and feed 'em." Sky offered his hand for a brief shake. "I'll see you at dinner, Kieran. Welcome to the family."

"Thanks."

Sara's dad stood. "If I won't be in the way, Sky, I'd like to come down to the barn with you and Buck. Maybe learn the ropes."

"It'd be great to have you."

"I'll head into the kitchen and get organized for the onslaught." Marybeth made her way down the hall.

"I'll be there soon," Desiree called after her as she motioned to Kieran. "First I need to show our honored guest where he's sleeping."

"I'll help you, Marybeth." Sara's mom got up from the couch.

"Me, too." Lani followed.

"Hey, Mom," Lucky took a step toward the kids' wing. "Are you putting Kieran in Rance's and my old room?"

"That was my plan."

"I'm coming, then. I want to show him some stuff. Oksana, do you—"

She chuckled and shook her head. "I've seen the room. Many times. Heard the stories."

"I'll tidy up here." Andy began gathering the remains of the drinks and snacks.

Sara went over to help, but he smiled and said he had it under control. Which left her with Oksana and Rance. She focused on him. "I take it you don't want to join Lucky and Kieran in your old bedroom?"

He snuck a peek at Andy, who was still loading the tray. "I'll let Lucky handle that. But I'm standing here wondering if anybody's figured out Kieran's suitcase, duffel or whatever he brought is still in his parked car back in town."

"I have," Oksana said, "but I doubt he has. Poor guy has to be shell-shocked by now."

"You know, he might not have locked it." Sara pictured the scene in Hannigan's. "He was exhausted from driving on the opposite side from what he's used to."

"Exactly." Rance looked at Oksana. "You could go ask him, and if it's open, somebody who's still in town could swing by and get his stuff. Like Clint, Tyra, Bret, Gil, even Jess if she's still at the newspaper office."

"I'll go check." She left for the kids' wing.

Sara gazed at her co-conspirator with a new level of respect. "Rance McLintock. You have the mind of an international spy."

"Thank you."

"I'm ready to put my fate in your hands. What's the plan?"

His eyes gleamed with a mixture of delight and mischief. "First of all, he can't stay here. I'm going to suggest that he stay in my cabin with me."

"But why? There's a sentimental value to him staying in Lucky's old room."

"Then both of you are stuck in a dormitory situation with zero chance you'll get horizontal without embarrassing yourselves and everybody else."

"But why your cabin? If he doesn't stay here, the next logical place is Lucky and Oksana's guest room."

"They're newlyweds. You notice Lucky didn't jump in to nix Mom's plan of him staying in our old room. He's thrilled to know Kieran exists, but he's also madly in love with his wife. He doesn't need to have his half-brother staying right across the hall."

"But you do? That makes no logical sense."

"It does if I want a chance to get to know him, one-on-one, without Lucky there."

"You do?"

"Think about it. For thirty years it's been Lucky and me, raised like twins, yin and yang. Now here comes this charming Irishman, who has an actual blood bond with Lucky. I'm suddenly...." He cast his gaze downward. "A fifth wheel."

"Oh, Rance. I'm so sor—"

"Not really." He looked up with an impish smile. "That's just how I'll sell it."

"You made that up?"

"Mostly. I could think of it that way if I wanted to, but I choose not to."

"Are you sure? Because I can see how this might be tough on you."

"Lucky and I were tested back in February. We're solid and this is awesome for him. Did I feel a twinge when I heard the news? Yeah, but I plucked out that barb and reminded myself that I'm Desiree McLintock's kid. I have her DNA and she's alive and effing amazing. I got the better end of the deal."

She took a deep breath. "That's a terrific attitude. And you've also generously dreamed up this elaborate scheme so Kieran and I can—"

"I'm not that selfless. But we'll get to that. There'll be smuggling involved and you'll have to get Lani to go along with it."

"That could be a problem. She's softening, but she still might not be willing to help."

"We need her, though. See what you can do. Once she's in, you and I will do a late-night switch so I sleep here and you sleep, or more likely don't sleep, at the cabin. We'll reverse it early in the morning."

"You'll take my bed in the room with Lani?"

"No. I wish, but no. I'll sleep in my old room."

"You wish? You have a crush on—"

"Yes, and if you tell her, I'll—"

"I won't, but listen, she'll never leave New Jersey."

Rance just smiled.

"I'm telling you, she won't. She loves that boutique publishing company she works for. Sure, she's delighted to find out your mom is a bestselling author, but it only gives them something in common. It doesn't change her career goals."

He shrugged. "That's a discussion for another day. What do you think of my plan? Should I ask Mom if Kieran can sleep in my guest room for the week he's here?"

"Do you even have a guest room? I seem to remember you shoved your sofa into your spare room to make room for a pool table."

"It so happens that's a sleeper sofa, but it doesn't matter because nobody's gonna sleep in the guest room. You and Kieran can have my room, complete with fresh sheets and a supply of condoms."

That thought made her shiver with anticipation. "How will we make the switch?"

"I'll drive my truck over here and you'll drive it back to my cabin."

"You'd trust me to drive Midnight Thunder?" Uneasiness curled in her stomach.

"You're up to it."

She gulped. "Okay." He had more confidence in that than she did. "How about Sam? Won't he hear your truck and come to investigate?"

"Mom closes him in the bedroom with her and Andy, especially when she has house guests who might get up in the middle of the night. She doesn't want Sam bothering them. Oh, and I'll find a moment before I leave tonight to oil the hinges on the front door."

She chuckled. "Methinks you've snuck out a few times in the past."

"There's an art to it."

"And I can tell you've mastered that art. But it's possible you'll take Kieran to your cabin and Lani will nix the whole program."

"In that case, I'll have a chance to bond with Kieran. It's not a terrible idea. By the way, I'll also tell Lucky and Oksana the plan. I don't want Lucky to think Kieran's arrival got my undies in a bunch."

"Good point. Oksana will be fine with the idea, but what about Lucky?"

"Are you kidding? After the big woolies he told so nobody would find out about his relationship with Oksana? He can't say a word."

"But with everybody here, you won't have a chance to—"

"Yes, I will. Lucky and Oksana will be giving me and Kieran a ride to my cabin."

"So they will. I forgot they picked you up from the Buffalo. You must have hitched a ride in with Clint."

"Serendipitously, I did. See how everything is falling into place?"

"I have to admit it's elegant. But you still haven't explained your motive. I'm guessing it has something to do with Lani, but I can't make the connection. What do you get out of this?"

"It's simple. If you rope Lani in, it means she's part of a secret, outrageous, yet manageable plan to help you and Kieran enjoy some private time. Sharing in something like that brings people closer. It makes their time together more memorable."

"Rance, please believe me, she won't move out here."

"Your folks are talking about it."

"Doesn't matter. She's got the life she wants in Trenton."

"So you say. Anyway, never mind about Lani. What about you? Think you'll ever live in Wagon Train?"

"No. Besides, it won't help me see Kieran more often. His visits here will likely be few and far between. It's expensive and I guarantee he won't let the McLintocks pay. I stand a better chance of seeing him if I stay where I am. Dublin to Newark is a cheaper flight."

He just gazed at her with that same maddening smile.

"Don't look at me like that. I'm right about this, damn it."

He sighed. "You need to start thinking outside the box, Miss Sara."

_15_

Kieran had always dreamed of being part of a big family. But he was unprepared for the holy show that engulfed him when the McLintocks gathered.

To be fair, it was mostly his fault. His unexpected appearance after thirty years had stirred the pot. And it was boiling over.

He'd been hugged so many times he had permanent creases in his shirt. His mouth was dry from constantly talking and he'd switched from beer to water so he wouldn't end up flat on his arse.

Could be this lot was trying to make up for thirty years in one go, judging from how keen they were to learn everything about him. His construction job got Angie and Kendall going and his mention of his favorite pub kicked off a long discussion with Clint and Tyra.

When Bret and Gil found out he'd done a spot of welding here and there, they latched right onto that subject. Cheyenne wanted to know if his village had a fire department and he had to disappoint that fella with the sad news they did not. Ella and Faye had better luck when they asked about the village schools, apart from the fact he hadn't been inside a classroom for years.

Being the star attraction in a large group wasn't easy and he wouldn't have made it through without Sara. She stuck by his side during the meet and greet and made sure she sat next to him when they moved the party to the long dining table.

He'd memorized the names of the adults but hadn't sorted the wee ones yet. Each of them perched in a highchair near the table, four girls and one boy, the oldest. That sturdy wee fella seemed to be best friends with a ginger girl about his age.

More babies were on the way, as well. With due dates next month Jess and Ella said they were ready to be done. Brit, only three months along and not showing at all, was the opposite, glowing with excitement as she talked about the baby girl she and Trent had already named Montana.

When everyone had settled and toasts had been made, he announced that he'd enjoy hearing about their lives for a change. He got more than he'd bargained for. He hadn't laughed so hard since... ever, not even when he and his mates got paralytic on whiskey.

Turned out the lot of them had the gift of storytelling, with pictures on their mobiles to prove it happened. The way Beau described racing his pigs left him roaring and gasping for breath. By the time the tale of the Christmas-themed condoms ended with a photo of a tree decorated with them, he was doubled over, tears streaming down his face.

Their parade of pictures reminded him to take some for Granny so he could text them to her in the morning. If only he could have magically transported her here for this dinner. She liked nothing better than sitting around a table sharing stories.

Desiree kept sending glances his way, like she was checking on him. As everyone polished off their dessert, she tapped her fork against her glass. "Kieran's had a very long day and it's time to wrap this up so he can hit the hay."

Old films from America had taught him what *hit the hay* meant. The idea suited him fine apart from one thing. He'd promised himself a kiss from Sara and he wasn't closing himself in Lucky's old bedroom without asking for a moment alone.

Chairs scraped back and conversation continued over the noise of clearing dishes from the table. He stood and picked up his plate, prepared to take it into the kitchen.

"I've got it, Kieran." A woman whisked it out of his hand. "You go relax."

He recognized the blue outfit. She was one of the Wenches, who'd all arrived wearing colors of the rainbow. She also had multicolored hair. Cindy? He'd chance it. "Thank you, Cindy."

"You're so welcome. Good memory." She beamed at him. "Sara, I've got yours, too." She took the plate Sara held. "You're our hero for steering this guy to Desiree. Well done."

"Thanks. I had no idea it would turn into something so... so...."

"Spectacular?"

"Yeah, that about covers it. I appreciate you taking our dishes."

"Glad to." With another big smile, she stacked the plates and picked up two more before hurrying away.

Sara touched his arm. "Follow me, I need to talk to you for a minute."

Just what he was hoping for. He didn't have talking in mind, but he'd follow her anywhere she led.

She lengthened her stride as she walked through the living room. "I'd like to make our escape before someone waylays us."

"Are we going outside?"

"No." Crossing the hall, she reached for the handle of a door that stood partway open. "In here."

He followed her into a room lined floor-to-ceiling with books. A rainbow of wingback chairs told him this might be where the Wenches hung out.

"Close the door."

"Happy to." Pulling it shut he studied the hardware.

"What are you doing?"

"Trying to find the lock."

She laughed. "We don't need to lock it. I didn't bring you in here to make out."

"If *make out* is what I think, that's exactly why I'm here." He turned around and found her only inches away. "If that's not what you're after, you'd better step back. Way back."

"I am after exactly that, but not now." She held her ground.

"Why not?"

"I have something important to tell you." Her breath came in quick little gasps. "If we start kissing, I won't get it said."

"Go on."

"Rance figured out how we can spend the night together."

The news smacked him in the chest and started his heart to racing. "*Tonight*?"

"Maybe, but I have to get Lani to go along with the idea, so we might have to wait until tomorrow night. Anyway, you'd probably fall asleep on me tonight if we—"

"I will *not* fall asleep on you. If you're saying there's a chance that we could—"

"Just be quiet and listen. Rance is talking to Desiree right now. He wants you to stay in his cabin this week instead of here at the house."

"Why?"

"So he and I can switch places after everyone's asleep. He'll be here for the night and I'll be in his cabin. With you."

His body hummed with anticipation. "How will you manage it?"

"He'll drive over here and I'll drive his truck back to the cabin. Before it gets light, I'll drive back here and he'll take his truck home again."

The thud of his heart echoed in his ears. It was a bold plan but it might work.

"But first Lani has to agree not to squeal on me. There's no way I could creep in and out of the room we're sharing without her waking up."

"Can you talk her into it?"

"I don't know. I'll do my best. This all hinges on my powers of persuasion."

"What if Desiree says no? I got the idea she really wants me to stay here."

"She probably does, but Rance will prevail."

"How do you know?"

"Ask him to explain it. Just go along with the plan to stay with him, okay?"

"I'd be a fool not to."

"I'll text Rance as soon as I know something one way or the other. Now we should get back out there."

"Without a kiss?"

"It's a bad idea."

He reached for her. "It's a very good—"

"We'll get carried away for sure and come out looking mussed and guilty." She laid a restraining hand on his chest. "Keep your eye on the prize."

He smiled. "Here's lookin' at you, kid."

"Aww. You've watched *Casablanca*."

"Yes, ma'am."

Her green eyes darkened. "I could eat you up with a spoon."

He pulled her closer. "Be my guest."

"No." She wiggled out of his arms. "We need to get out there and not show our hand by looking flushed. Which I probably already am."

"You're stunning."

"You're not helping." She took a deep breath. "Tell you what. You go out first and I'll wait a while. If anyone questions what you were doing in here, tell them you love libraries."

"That I do. And bookshops. And the smell of old books. My brother and I have that in common."

"I don't know how you do it, but you just get sexier with every word that comes out of your mouth."

"That's good news."

"Now vamoose."

"Yes, ma'am." He gave her a wink before he turned on his heel and walked out the door, his step light. She wanted him bad enough to go along with Rance's elaborate plan. It might even work. It might even work tonight.

He needed coffee. Strong coffee.

_16_

The plan was in motion. Rance's convincing story had worked and at this very moment Lucky and Oksana were giving Kieran and Rance a lift to Rance's cabin. And getting an earful. Sara would have loved to listen in on that conversation.

Were they speculating on whether Lani would go along with the scheme? Sara wanted that answer, too, but she wouldn't get it until she was tucked into the privacy of the bedroom they shared.

That might not happen for a while. Angie, Dallas, Brit and Trent had stayed on after the rest had left. So had Margaret, Brit's mom. The whole Armstrong family hadn't been together since February and Brit's pregnancy gave them plenty to talk about.

Desiree and Andy served the Bailey's Sara's parents had brought as a house gift and everyone gathered around the fireplace. The evening was chilly enough for a modest fire and Dallas tended it, gently feeding the flames to provide atmosphere without overheating the room.

Under different circumstances, Sara would have relaxed into the moment. Dallas crouched near the hearth nursing a fire reminded her of all the times her big brother had appropriated the job back home.

Trent's happy smile had returned after years of misery, and that was wonderful to see. Her earlier fears that the situation with Brit would be a trainwreck had disappeared. He was head-over-heels and Brit clearly returned his love. They'd make great parents.

Everyone was so relaxed and happy that guilt pricked her. Sneaking around wasn't her normal behavior, but this cozy setup with her parents and her sister in the kids' wing of the ranch house created a virtual chastity belt.

It wasn't like she and Kieran could take a rain check, either. It was now or never. Rance's scheme was her only alternative for satisfying their longing for each other without creating a ruckus. Even one night of bliss was worth the risk.

Her dad had brought a mocktail version of Bailey's for Brit, and Sara would have preferred that. But doing anything out of the ordinary wasn't a good idea so she'd taken a small glass of the regular stuff and was drinking it slowly.

She'd need all her resources to drive that big black truck if by some miracle Lani bought into the plan. Rance must really believe this caper would win him points with Lani if he was willing to risk Midnight Thunder.

"By the way, Sara." Desiree glanced at her. "I didn't want to say anything while Kieran was here, but fixing that headstone won't be as easy as

I imagined. We'd be better off just getting a new one."

"How long would that take?"

"Weeks. Maybe longer. It was probably the same time frame when I ordered the other one, but I was too busy with Rance and Lucky to notice. That's been my only experience. Angie's dad was buried in a family plot back East. I had no idea you couldn't just get one in a few days."

"One of our dental patients advised me to take care of everything now," Margaret said. "And not leave it for Brit. Great advice. Have I done it? No."

"Same." Sara's mom lifted her glass in Margaret's direction. "My parents have everything organized and prepaid. Sadly, Harry and I have made zero preparations for our eventual demise."

"I'm glad we haven't," her dad said. "The way things are going, you and I will be planted right here."

"That's terrific news, Dad." Dallas beamed at them.

"Don't get too excited, son. Your mom and I don't plan on kicking off anytime soon."

"That isn't what I meant. I just—"

"I know. You're eager for us to make the move. I guess this is the time to announce that we're meeting with a real estate agent when we get home. The house will be on the market by next month."

"Woo-hoo!" Brit lifted her glass. "That deserves a toast. To Grandpa Harry and Grandma Vanessa moving to Montana!"

Sara touched glasses with everyone she could reach and ignored the twinge of sadness. Her childhood home would soon belong to strangers. She'd been in the habit of dropping by for dinner at least once a week.

Sometimes she and Lani had coordinated so they'd both be there. She glanced at her sister, who met her gaze and gave a little shrug, like *what can you do?*

"The market's hot right now, Dad," Trent said. "What if the house sells right away? Have you decided where you'll—"

"Oh, that. Desiree says we'll always have our room here. Or we can live with you and Brit, or Dallas and Angie."

"Oh." Trent exchanged a look of panic with Dallas.

"I kind of like the idea of floating between the two places, fancy free, no lawn to mow, no roof to repair, no taxes to pay. We'd kick in for groceries, and—"

"Harry, stop it." Their mom gave him a swat. "Your boys are freaking out. We're not living with you guys. Or Desiree. She tried to give us land but we forced her to take money for it. We'll be building a cabin on Rowdy Ranch."

Both couples let out a collective sigh of relief.

"And," their mother continued, "instead of hiring a contractor, Angie, we'd like to hire you and Kendall."

"Wow!" Her eyes widened. "We accept! I can't wait to tell Kendall. We've talked about whether we could handle an entire house. I think we can."

"Harry and I have every confidence in you two."

Desiree let out a happy sigh. "I love how this is working out. Is it wrong of me to want all of you to come live here?"

Andy gave her a smile. "It's not right or wrong, Dez. It's just you. You want to gather all your chicks under your wing."

"So true. But don't mind me, Lani and Sara. I understand that you have jobs you love and friends you care about."

"But it's sweet of you to want us," Lani said.

Sara nodded. "And we'll visit a lot more if Mom and Dad are living here."

"I'll look forward to that. Now if only Kieran... but that's much more complicated. Sure would be great, though, especially for Lucky."

"He's not the only one," Angie said. "Kendall and I want to hire him."

Desiree's eyes lit up. "Did you ask him?"

"Not yet, but Wagon Train Handywomen needs another person, especially if we're going to expand into home construction. We've been quietly looking around. Then along comes Kieran. He'd be perfect."

Brit grinned. "You might want to reconsider the name."

"We've already thought of one. We'd become Two Handywomen and a Dude. If we drop Wagon Train from the name we can go after business in nearby towns."

Desiree's eyebrows rose. "Trying to keep up with Lucky?"

Angie just smiled.

"I love it." Brit looked at Trent. "What's our resident marketing expert think?"

"I say go for it. Only make it Two Handywomen and a Cowboy."

"Except he isn't one," Lani said. "He told me he's never been on a horse."

"Minor detail. He's already bought the hat. I guarantee someone will get him on a horse this week." Trent looked straight at Sara.

She took a breath. "It's an exciting idea."

"You're not crazy about it, though," Angie said. "Why not?"

"I just think... he might want to do it, but I can't imagine him leaving his grandmother and it doesn't sound like she'd come with him."

"I'd completely understand if that's his choice. You could be right that she won't budge."

"I'm only going by what he's said."

"Then you think if I offered him a job, I might put him between a rock and a hard place?"

"Kind of. Yeah."

"I won't mention it yet. I'll tell Kendall not to say anything, either. We'll see how the next few days go."

Sara's anxiety eased. "That sounds good." Angie's offer could absolutely put him in a bind. The McLintocks were a dazzling bunch. But his granny was his top priority. His loyalty to her was one of the things that made him special.

"Now that we have that semi-settled and the fire's almost out..." Dallas polished off his

Bailey's and stood. "We should probably shove off, honeybunch."

"Yep. Sure was nice to hang out, though." Angie got up, too. "Looks like we'll all be here for Christmas."

"I have Harry and Vanessa's solid promise," Desiree said, "so if Lani and Sara can—"

"Oh, we'll be here. Right, sis?" Lani glanced at her.

"Yep. Wouldn't miss it."

The gathering broke up after Dallas and Angie left. Within twenty minutes, Sara was headed down the hall with Lani.

She gave her sister dibs on the hall bathroom they shared. If the discussion went as she hoped, she wouldn't be changing into her PJs tonight.

As she sat on her bed and waited for Lani's return, she went over her pitch, but a little voice in her head kept distracting her. Was she also putting Kieran in a bind?

While she was wrestling with that, Lani came back in wearing her pjs.

"The bathroom's all yours." She tucked her clothes in a laundry bag.

"I have something I need to talk to you about."

Turning, Lani gazed at her. "I knew it. Rance has been acting weird. You're acting weird. He kidnapped Kieran. What are you guys up to?"

Sara told her.

"Oh, good Lord! Rance expects you to drive his big truck for the first time on the ranch roads by yourself at night?"

"Yes, but that's not the part that worries me."

"It's the part that worries *me*. I don't—"

"Then you don't object to the idea of me and Kieran—"

"Look, I've been watching you two and you'll find a way before the week is over. I'd rather you guys are in a safe spot and supplied with condoms instead of out in the woods with the bears and playing Russian roulette with your cycle."

"I wouldn't have risked getting pregnant."

"Okay, but don't pretend you wouldn't sneak into the woods with him because you've already done it once. And he's from Ireland. He knows less about bears than we do."

"Then you like this plan?"

"I wouldn't say *like*, but it's okay, except the truck-driving part."

"There's no other way to work it, but that's not why I'm hesitating. I'm afraid I'll—"

"There is another way. Rance can come here, get you, drop you at his cabin and then drive back here to spend the night. Then he can do it in reverse before dawn."

"That's so many extra trips. Extra time and extra gas. I can't ask him to do that."

"I can and I will. That's the only way I'm greenlighting this thing. You're a good driver but that truck is massive and there are no streetlights or signs out here."

"But—"

"I wouldn't risk it myself and I'm sure as hell not going along with a plan that puts you in that position. I'll be happy to call him and say so." She reached for her phone on the nightstand between the beds.

"You have his number?"

"Only because he grabbed my phone when I had it open and added himself. I just haven't taken the time to delete it. And his texts are kind of funny."

"Wait. Don't call him. I'm not even sure I should go."

"Why not?"

"What if he falls in love with me? But he can't leave Ireland? Then I've put him in a bind, just like I was worried Angie would with her job offer."

"What if you fall in love with him?"

"I sort of have already. But I'm prepared. I can handle it."

Lani rolled her eyes.

"I *can*. I just don't know if he's thought it through. Also, he's gotta be exhausted. I need to call him. For starters, we probably should postpone this until tomorrow night."

"Then call him." Lani flopped back on her bed. "If you decide to go for it, have him put Rance on." She blew out a breath. "I can't believe he expects you to drive Thunder. What was he thinking? Oh, yeah. I keep forgetting. He's crazy."

<u>17</u>

Kieran had downed one mug of black coffee and would have another after Rance gave him a few tips on his pool game. Didn't fancy being scundered the first time he played at Rowdy Roost.

He chose a cue from the rack and stepped over to the grand table that took up most of Rance's living room.

"You played in your local pub, right?" Rance rubbed chalk on the tip of his cue.

"Yeah, some, but mostly darts. Our tables are smaller. And the—" His mobile chimed and leprechauns danced in his gut. *Sara.* He laid his cue on the table and reached in his pocket.

Rance put down his cue, folded his arms and looked at him.

"This is it." He tapped the screen and put the phone to his ear. "Hello, Sara."

"Kieran, we need to talk."

That confused the hell out of him. "Did you ask Lani? What did—"

"She's okay with the plan but she—"

"She is?" He gave Rance a thumbs up and got one in return.

"She doesn't want me driving the truck by myself."

"I don't fancy that part, either. I wish—"

"Kieran, I'm worried."

"About driving Midnight Thunder?"

"The truck's minor. I'm worried about how this... whatever we choose to call it... could impact you."

"Meaning?"

"You could become... attached to me."

"I'm already attached to you. I can tell you're attached to me. We should do something about it."

"Maybe attached is the wrong word."

"I like it." He smiled. "Connected is another good word."

Rance mouthed *What the hell?* and lifted both hands, palms up.

"The point is, we might see each other again if I go to Dublin for work, but there's no guarantee."

"Oh, it's guaranteed. If you come within a thousand kilometers, I'll make sure we see each other."

"You will?"

"You'll be crossing that ocean sometime. It's part of your job."

"But it might not be convenient. You might have a girlfriend."

"I'll still want to see you. You were with me on the most important day of my life. I don't intend for us to lose touch. It's not all about sex, although I wouldn't mind adding that to the mix."

Rance made a circling motion with his hand, which meant *wrap it up* in any language.

"It sounds different when you put it that way, but..." She trailed off.

Time to face this head on. "What's bothering you?"

"What if you fall in love with me? What if you can't imagine life without me?"

He sucked in a breath. "I'm already half in love with you. I can't imagine the world without you in it. Do I see us spending the rest of our lives together? I'm not an eejit."

"Oh, Kieran, that's not what—"

"We should probably decide about tonight, though. Rance is staring at the ceiling and tapping his foot."

She made a funny sound, half laugh and half gulp. "I want to come over. But first Lani has to talk to Rance. Could you please put him on?"

"I'll do that." He held out the phone. "Lani wants to talk to you, mate."

"She does?" His expression switched from bored to highly alert. "Hey, Lani. What do you—"

Kieran couldn't hear exactly what Lani was saying, but her delivery was forceful.

"In my defense, it's an automatic with power steering. Once she adjusts the seat, she'll be—"

Another torrent of words from Lani.

"I've never heard of a bear chasing a truck for the tasty people inside. The bear wouldn't win that race. My truck can outrun a bear."

He stared at the floor and listened some more. "A flat could happen. That's why they invented cell phones. But hey, you're right." He lifted his head and gave Kieran a long-suffering look. "That's how we'll do it."

Kieran murmured *how soon?*

"What time should I drive over? Can you tell whether your folks are..." He rolled his eyes. "No, I'm not suggesting you go listen at their door. Geez." He made a face.

Kieran wrote a three, a zero and a question mark in the air.

"How about thirty minutes? Would that be enough time for things to settle down?" He gave a quick nod. "Okay I'll be there in thirty. Yes, ma'am. My pleasure. Good night." He handed back the phone. "She hung up, so I hope you and Sara got things worked out."

"They've been worked out on my end from the first time I saw her. I'll take whatever Sara offers and expect no more."

"I admire you for that. I suck at stoicism."

Kieran grinned and gestured toward the pool table, it's green felt and dark carved wood glowing in light from the chandelier suspended over it. "Never could've guessed it, mate."

"Okay, so we've got twenty-five minutes. What part of your game do you want to work on?"

"There's no way I'll keep my mind on pool."

Rance shrugged. "No worries. We can do this another time." He picked up both cues and returned them to the rack. Then he rolled the balls into the pockets. "Want more coffee?"

"I thought I did, but that phone call was like a shot of jet fuel." He gazed at Rance. "How well do you know Sara?"

"Fairly well, considering I only spent a few days with her and Lani in February, but we clicked. We're a lot alike. She's spontaneous, likes people, likes to have fun, has a good heart. We get each other."

Was that a twinge of jealousy? He had no right to feel that. "So you're good friends, then?"

"If you're asking if I've kissed her, the answer is no."

"Jaysus, mate! I wasn't thinking of *that*." But he was. Exactly that. "Why not? She's a stunner."

"I would agree." Rance walked over to one of the tall stools lining the walls and perched on it. "Last February I seriously thought about making a move. There was a spark, an attraction, but it would have been a mistake to kiss her."

"Why?" He leaned his hip against the pool table, too jumpy to sit down.

"I was still waffling. It's bad enough I've danced with both of them. Flirted, too. You can't do that with sisters. I learned the hard way. You need to pick one, and once you do, the other one's off-limits."

"You might eventually pick Sara?" He braced himself. He had to be okay with her ending up with somebody else. Wouldn't he rather have it be someone he knew? No. He'd prefer a nameless, faceless stranger.

"I wouldn't have set this up for you if that was a possibility. It's not. I've made my choice."

He sagged in relief. "Lani?"

"Yessir. If you'd gone after her, you wouldn't have a snowball's chance in hell of getting near that lady. I would've seen to it."

"Does she know?"

He shook his head. "Sara does, but she won't say anything."

"Nor me."

"I know that. It's easy to tell you're solid."

"Is talking to Lani face-to-face part of this plan? You're gonna knock on her door and—"

"God, no. That would be a full-blown disaster."

"Or a golden opportunity."

"It's not time yet."

"How do you know?"

"I just do. She's not ready to hear what I have to say. And I'm not ready to say it. When she comes for Christmas, I will be."

"That's four months away! She could be engaged to some chancer in New Jersey by then. She's a right feek, in case you haven't noticed."

He laughed. "A right feek? "

"It means she's nice to look at."

"In that case, yes, I've noticed. I just don't want her to figure that out. Not yet."

"You're not going to show your hand?"

That made him grin. "Keeping my cards close to my vest. And a few up my sleeve."

"You do remind me of that fella Maverick. Granny loves that old show. But you're taking a risk to wait like that."

"And you're taking one by charging ahead."

He dragged in a breath. "That I am." He let it out slowly. "And it's worth taking."

_**18**_

Creeping through the dark house in her sock feet, her heart thumping, Sara expected to be caught any minute. She carried her phone, a jeans jacket and her boots, so pretending to be after a drink of water wasn't an option.

If someone switched on a light and asked where she was going, she'd claim that there was a meteor shower she was eager to see and maybe photograph. Then she'd have to pray she could text Rance in time to have him hold up until she gave him the all-clear.

Her tennis shoes would have been easier to carry than boots, but Lani had insisted on the boots for getting in and out of the truck in the dark. Sara hadn't argued, because her sister was right.

A ranch in Montana was nothing like the area where they'd grown up. She'd only seen one reptile in her neighborhood, a cute little garter snake in the back yard. And no bears, obviously.

Snakes and bears hadn't been an issue in February, but Desiree had been clear that everyone kept their eyes open this time of year. She'd advised using the flashlight on their phone if they were walking around after dark.

Lani had reminded her about using the flashlight once she was out on the porch. As a little kid, she used to yell *you're not the boss of me* when Lani issued reminders, or worse yet, tried to stop her from doing something. Now she cherished Lani's protectiveness.

If their roles had been reversed, Sara would have worried about Lani driving Rance's truck alone in the dark. These days they took care of each other, especially when one of them was flooded with hormones and might not be thinking clearly.

She was awash in them right now, shaky with anticipation laced with disbelief. Could this wild scheme actually work?

The front door wasn't locked. Doors seldom were on this ranch. The custom came in handy tonight, since she had no way to lock it behind her. It opened silently on its well-oiled hinges.

Stepping into the cool air, she pulled the door closed. A breeze rustled the leaves of the trees that surrounded the house, making her jump.

White fairy lights in the trees danced and sparkled, giving her a decent view of the area. No sign of bears. Crickets chirped in the bushes and a crescent moon dangled above the dark bulk of the Sapphire Mountains.

She put on her boots and her jacket. In preparation for this rendezvous, she'd taken time for a quick shower and a change of clothes.

In the distance, a faint purr slowly grew to a soft rumble. Headlights flashed briefly as Rance's black truck slowly rounded the curve. He shut those off, leaving only the parking lights on.

Then he cut the engine and Midnight Thunder rolled down the slight incline toward the house, stopping a few yards from the front porch.

Her chest tight and her movements jerky, she managed to tap the flashlight on her phone and scanned the ground ahead as she hurried down the steps.

He met her halfway, the light from his phone also directed at the ground. "I have an idea."

If he hadn't been right in front of her, she wouldn't have heard his low murmur. "What?"

"You should drive."

Her breath caught. "Why?"

"Because it's fun. You'll like it. And with me there, you won't be scared. Wanna do it?"

She glanced up at him and grinned. "Yeah."

"I'll walk you to the driver's side and get you situated."

"Okay." She fell into step beside him as they approached the open driver's door. "Why isn't the dome light on?"

"I turned it off before I drove over. An extra precaution."

"You're wasting your talents working as a bartender. You should be a CIA operative."

"Nah. Doesn't fit into my life plan."

"You have one?"

"Absolutely. Climb on up and I'll adjust the seat."

She swung up behind the leather-covered wheel and settled into the cushy seat. "Ready."

"Tell me when." The seat moved with a soft whine.

"That's good."

"I'll be right there." He gently pushed the door closed.

While he came around to the passenger side, she snapped on her seatbelt and surveyed the dashboard. It was more high-tech than her car at home, but she could probably figure it out. And wow, the view out the windshield was awesome.

Rance hopped in and quietly pulled the passenger side door closed. "So how do you like Thunder so far?"

"I love him. Sitting up so high is fantastic. If I had this in Trenton, I'd rule the Black Dragon."

"That's the New Jersey Turnpike, right?"

"Right."

"You drive it?"

"Sure."

"Does Lani?"

"Of course."

"That's crazy. You're way safer driving Thunder on ranch roads than risking your life on that turnpike."

"Probably. Except like now, when the snakes and bears are roaming around...."

"Yeah, I get it. The chance of you having to deal with either is minimal, but it's better if I'm with you."

"Sorry about the gas. I'll chip in for the extra."

"No, ma'am."

"But—"

"Time to get going. We don't want to be caught sitting out here chit-chatting. And Kieran's likely worn a groove in my porch floorboards by now. Any questions?"

"Not yet." She started the engine and put the truck in reverse. "How touchy is the gas pedal?"

"Touchy. Easy does it."

She stepped lightly on the pedal and gradually added more pressure until the big truck began to move. Using the backup camera, she turned it around until they faced the ranch road. "Thunder's huge, but he handles like a dream."

"Having fun?"

"I am." She shifted into drive and used the parking lights until she rounded the bend in the road. Then she paused and switched on the headlights.

Something small and furry ran across the road. Then a second one followed but stopped halfway to turn and look at the truck, its glowing eyes framed by a black mask.

"Raccoons! How adorable!"

"And that's why we creep along the ranch roads, especially at night in the summer."

"I've been so fixated on the scary critters I didn't stop to think you'd have cute ones out here, too."

"I love 'em all." He peered through the windshield. "I think it was just those two. You can keep going but stay alert."

"Don't worry, I will." As she gave the truck gas she focused on the road ahead. "Do you really love them all?"

"I do."

"How about big hairy spiders?"

"They're cool. We need spiders in this world. Hey, in a little bit, you'll hit the main ranch road. Take a left."

"Got it." She doubted Rance loved every living thing. Everybody had some critter they disliked. At the intersection, she braked, checked for animals, and made the turn. "Mosquitoes. You can't love them."

"They're food for bats and I love bats."

"Cockroaches."

"Again, food for other creatures and they also really shine in the forest, where they clean up dead leaves and debris and leave valuable nitrogen behind."

"I've never met anyone who advocated for cockroaches."

He chuckled. "Well, now you have. I'm a circle-of-life guy and I get to see it in action out here. I need to be close to this land, the plants and the critters or I'll shrivel up and die."

He was serious about that, too. She'd never seen this side of Rance. "Then can I give you some advice?"

"Like what?"

"Don't set your sights on Lani."

"Too late."

"It'll never work. Aside from the fact she hates roaches, she craves the intellectual energy of the East Coast as much as you crave the natural beauty of Montana."

"Are you saying I have about as much chance of ending up with Lani as you have ending up with Kieran?"

"That's what I'm saying."

"Then I'm better off than I thought."

"You're making no sense."

"And you're almost to my cabin. Slow down."

She gulped. Their discussion had temporarily sidetracked her libido, but it snapped to attention as lights shining through the trees pinpointed the location of Rance's cabin.

A wave of longing washed through her, leaving her moist and achy.

Kieran was there. Waiting.

<u>19</u>

The rumble of Midnight Thunder's engine brought Kieran's pacing to an abrupt end. His coiled muscles tightened another notch. Holding his breath, he waited, fists clenched, for lights to appear on the road.

He hadn't checked the time when Rance left, but an eternity had passed since then. Which meant the plan had been banjaxed. He just knew it. Lani had changed her mind. Or Sara had. Or she'd been discovered sneaking out. Or—

Headlights flashed through the trees. The beams swerved as Rance made the turn and drove toward the cabin. Was he alone? Blinded by the glare, Kieran couldn't tell. The lights stayed on as the engine cut off and both doors opened.

Both doors. He focused on the passenger side as... Rance? If he wasn't driving, then who the hell was? His attention flew to the driver's side. Sara hopped down, her smile outshining those headlights.

He took the steps in a single bound. "You drove?"

"I did!" She threw up both hands in triumph. "And we saw raccoons and I—"

He smothered the rest with a kiss born of joy, frustration and a flood of relief.

She kissed him back, opening her mouth to his tongue, sliding her arms around him and holding on as if she'd never let go. He didn't want her to. Might as well just pick her up and carry her into — the sound of a throat being cleared, then cleared again, finally penetrated the lust that had turned his brain to porridge.

Oh, yeah. Rance. Still here. Lifting his head, he looked to his left, and sure enough, the fella who'd engineered this entire event stood facing them watching the show, hands shoved in his pockets, a smug smile on his face.

He deserved to be smug. He deserved to be properly thanked, too. "Hey, mate." He sucked in a lungful of air. "Thank you. Doesn't seem like enough just to say that, but—"

"Thank you from me, too, Rance." Sara looked over at him but she didn't loosen her hold. "I owe you one."

"And I'll collect someday. I'm glad to see you both so happy." He tipped his head toward the front door, which stood slightly ajar. "Remember to close that after you go in."

Kieran nodded. "I will." He'd left it that way on purpose. He'd be sure to close it behind him now that he'd been reminded. If Rance had slipped away without saying anything, that door might've stood open all night. He'd been just that focused on the situation at hand.

"See you in the morning." Rance touched the brim of his hat. "Four-thirty."

"*Four-thirty*?" Sara's response came out as a squeak of protest.

"Or I could stay at the ranch for breakfast and explain the setup to the folks. Your choice."

She let out a sigh. "Four-thirty it is. You're a good friend for getting up at that godawful hour. And for letting me drive your truck."

"You're welcome." He walked around to the driver's side and fiddled with something that made a humming sound.

"He has to put the seat back," Sara murmured. "He adjusted it for me."

"Why did you end up driving?" Although he desperately wanted to kiss her again, he'd hold off until Rance left.

"He thought I'd like it."

He envied the fella's close friendship with Sara. But without it, they wouldn't have this time together. "Did you like it?"

"Not as much as I like this." She snuggled closer and gazed up at him in a silent invitation.

"I'm waitin' for Rance to saunter on."

Her green eyes sparkled. "Then we can get down to business?"

"Yes, ma'am."

The sparkle deepened to a glow. "You have no idea how saying that turns me on."

"Yeah, I do. I can see it in your eyes." Midnight Thunder's engine turned over. Not long, now. "You won't be needing this." He slid the jacket from her shoulders.

"Sure won't." She let go of him long enough to pull her arms out of the sleeves.

"I'll take it." Laying it over his shoulder, he gathered her close, her body heat melting his resistance. He might need to kiss her, after all.

She raised the stakes, adjusting her hips to put pressure on his willy. "Your eyes just changed, too."

"That's not all that's changing." Tires crunched on gravel as Rance put Midnight Thunder in reverse. Not long, now.

"I know." She wiggled a bit. "Feels promising."

"Keep doing that and we won't make it past the porch." Tires scraped up more gravel as Rance continued backing in a half-circle. After a pause to switch gears, he pulled away from the cabin.

Gone. Slipping the leash on his body's urgent demands, Kieran cupped Sara's arse and lifted her off her feet.

Her breath caught. "Are you going to ravish me, Kieran Haggerty?"

"That I am." He tightened his grip and turned toward the cabin.

She clung to him, wrapping her legs around his hips as he bolted up the steps and shouldered his way through the front door. He'd known it would be like this. Known he wouldn't have the patience to turn a doorknob.

A swift nudge with the toe of his boot and the door swung closed.

She lifted her face to his. "Am I too heavy?"

"Never." He lengthened his stride as he crossed the living room. Good thing he'd turned back the covers, dimmed the lights and laid a condom on the bedside table.

"You're panting."

"I'm that excited to lie with you." The fire in his loins burned hot, hotter than he ever remembered.

"I want you, too. Deep inside me."

With a groan, he barreled through the bedroom door and laid her crossways on the bed. Tossing her jacket aside, he followed her down, his body covering hers.

His mouth sought the lips he craved while his fingers curled around the hem of her 'T-shirt. Breaking away from the kiss, he yanked the shirt upward. She lifted her arms so he could pull it over her head.

He gasped in delight. No bra. "You do flush all over." And he couldn't get enough of looking at her beautiful breasts, her nipples tight with passion. "Thank you for not wearing your—"

"That's not all I'm not wearing." Her voice was breathy and trembling with eagerness. "Take off my boots. After that, it's clear sailing."

He didn't have to be told twice. Pushing away from the bed, he pulled off her boots. When he straightened, she'd stretched out lengthwise, allowing him to see that what he'd thought were jeans were leggings that he could pull right off. When he tugged them away, her socks came with them.

He froze, stunned speechless by the woman lying there. His fantasy.

His only one. He'd dreamed of her countless times, stretched out on a bed in a softly lit room, her ginger hair bright against the white pillowcase. *He'd found her*. Dear God in heaven, he'd found her.

"Is something wrong?"

"Oh, no. Something's very right." He dragged in a breath. "So right it scares me." He began stripping off his clothes. No wonder she'd looked familiar when he'd first seen her in Hannigan's.

"You look like you've seen a ghost."

"Not a ghost. An angel."

"I'm no angel."

"You look like one to me." Had the fairies been at work here? He kept his attention on Sara's luminous, sensual body as if she might evaporate before his eyes.

He'd accepted so many amazing events today as true, but this… making love to someone right out of his dreams….

Was he so knackered that he was hallucinating? Had he been dreaming this entire day?

No. *No*, by God. He'd made it to Wagon Train. He'd learned his mother's fate. He'd discovered his half-brother.

And in this surreal moment, he was hard as a shillelagh, aching for the woman gazing at him, a smile on her kiss-reddened lips.

"That's what I'm talking about." She grabbed the condom from the bedside table and tossed it to him.

He made a one-handed catch without breaking eye contact. Ripping open the package, he suited up while keeping her in sight. Clearly he'd watched *Ladyhawke* too many times with Granny.

As he approached the bed, she opened her arms. "So serious, my sweet Irishman."

Her voice... even that was familiar. But climbing into bed with her was not. He'd never made love to the woman of his dreams.

If he was imagining this moment, then he'd wake up any second now. He moved between her silken thighs, the brush of her soft skin making him shiver with longing.

Poised at the entrance to paradise, he leaned down and kissed her gently. "I want you so much I'm shaking."

"I'm shaking, too." She stroked his chest and flattened her palm over his beating heart. "It's going so fast."

Lifting his head, he looked into her shamrock green eyes. "I keep thinking you'll disappear."

"I won't." Her eyes darkened and she wrapped her arms around him. "Make love to me, Kieran."

"Yes, ma'am." He plunged into her warm, welcoming body with the certainty that she would change his life.

20

Sara hadn't been prepared, not prepared at all, for a surge of pleasure so strong she cried out.

Kieran went completely still. "Did I hurt you, lass?"

"No! That was a cry of pure joy."

"Pure joy, is it, then?" He held her gaze and a slow smile curved his sexy mouth. "That's good news." Easing back, he pushed forward again. "Still good?"

"Uh-huh." A quiver in her lady parts promised fun times ahead. "I think you got this party started."

"Then let's keep it going." He began an easy rhythm.

Simple. And oh, so effective. His eyes were a mesmerizing blue as he continued the most intimate caress of all. Nothing fancy. And yet... he slowly, almost without effort, was turning her inside out.

The finale, when it came, was swift. One minute she was gliding along on a wave of pleasant sensation and the next she was flung over Niagara Falls, yelling and holding on for dear life.

He kept thrusting, prolonging the best damned climax she'd ever had. Gradually he tapered off until at last he stopped moving.

She took a shaky breath. "How... how did you do that?"

"Changed the angle a bit."

"That was the most spectacular sex I've ever had."

His eyebrows rose. "You don't usually—"

"Oh, I have orgasms, but nobody's ever... you have skills, my friend. And you didn't come."

"Because I think you can come again." He settled in deeper.

Sure enough, whatever angle he'd found was still sensitive to that measured rhythm and in no time she was tossed over the edge into the swirling waters of another spectacular climax.

Only this time he joined her, his breathing rougher than before and his strokes faster. Throwing back his head, he called her name in a hoarse shout of triumph. Then he pushed deep, gasping for air as his body shuddered against hers.

She rubbed his back until he stopped trembling. When he lowered his head, his eyes were closed. He murmured something she couldn't hear.

Then he opened his eyes and looked directly into hers. "Marry me."

"*What*?" The shock of it left her gasping.

He sighed. "You think I'm acting the maggot. And I probably—"

"If that means you're acting crazy, then yes, you are. We had wonderful sex, but that doesn't—"

"I know." Grasping the base of his cock to keep the condom secure, he eased away from her and left the bed. "I'll be right back. We'll talk."

"There's nothing to talk about!" She fought panic. Her worst fear was coming true. One fabulous sexual experience and he was head-over-heels in love with her.

And now she was going to hurt him. She couldn't bear to hurt him, but what choice did she have now that he had this insane idea fixed in his besotted brain?

She should call off this arrangement immediately. Staying in this cabin with him for another minute would only make things worse.

Except she was stuck here, wasn't she? She couldn't call Rance and ask him to take her back. She could at least get dressed, though. Climbing out of bed, she surveyed the array of clothes strewn across the floor.

"Searching for your clothes, are you?"

She glanced up. Why did he have to be so gorgeous? And good in bed? She couldn't look at his magnificent body without wanting more of what he'd just given her.

"Please don't get dressed."

"We can't make love anymore. You're falling for me. We talked about this on the phone, and you said—"

"That I didn't see us spending the rest of our lives together. I know."

"And an hour later you're asking me to marry you?"

"An hour ago I didn't know what I was talking about." His warm gaze swept over her. "I didn't know who you were, lass."

She groaned. "You know that's crazy talk, right?"

"Just let me explain what—"

"I know you're crazy, but then you give me that look and call me *lass*. And I want you all over again! It's not fair, Kieran."

"Come back to bed. We'll work this out."

"We're *not* making love. Not when you—"

"We're not. I need my wits about me for this discussion."

"Okay, then." She walked around the foot of the bed, propped a pillow against the headboard and got in. "This is my side." She pulled the sheet up and tucked it under her armpits. "You need to stay on your side."

"All right."

"It's not funny."

"It will be some day. You'll see."

"I doubt it."

He copied her setup except he only pulled the sheet up to his waist, the rat. His lovely broad chest with its sprinkling of soft chest hair was on full display. But asking him to cover it would sound ridiculous.

He took a deep breath. "Remember when I said I was afraid you'd disappear?"

"Yes."

"Have you ever seen *Ladyhawke*?"

"It's my favorite mov— wait! Did you think I'd turn into a hawk?"

"Something like that. I never expected to find you. And when I did, I had trouble believing you were real, since I've only seen you in my dreams."

She hadn't meant to look at him, but when he came out with a statement like that, she couldn't help it. "I'm your dream girl?"

"Yes." His gaze remained steady.

"In what way?"

"Every way. When I first saw your face in the mirror at Hannigan's, you looked familiar, but I knew I hadn't met you before since you've never been to Ireland. Then tonight I saw you lying on the bed and I finally recognized you. In my dreams you're always naked."

"You really believe that somehow I'm the incarnation of your dream girl?"

"That I do. I wasn't positive until we made love."

"You made love to me in your dreams?"

"I never did. I guess that part had to wait until we were physically together. It was the final proof."

"So let me get this straight. I look something like your dream girl, so—"

"Exactly like."

"Okay, I'm the spitting image of her."

He frowned. "I don't know what spit has to do with—"

"Never mind. I look like her, so based on that, you think we should get married."

"Hell, no. It goes way deeper than that. It's all the circumstances that brought us together. I've been working for years to get to Wagon Train. I could have come any week, but I came this week. You could have ended up here any week but your family chose this one. I decide to get a hat, walk into that shop, and there you were."

"Coincidence."

"Is it? We were instantly attracted to each other. Have you ever had that kind of reaction to someone?"

"No, but—"

"Neither have I. And for a while it looked like we'd never be able to act on it. Then Rance came up with a solution and here we are."

She took several slow breaths while she sorted through all he'd said. "It's a very romantic picture you've painted, but if you're thinking I'll just move to Ireland and live in your little village, that's not happening."

"But you said your company is international. They must have an office in Dublin."

"They do, but they also have a strict policy of hiring only people native to the country for the local offices."

"So you'd have to leave your job."

"Yes."

"I wouldn't ask you to do that."

"And I wouldn't ask you to leave your granny!"

"Good, because I would never do that."

"So even if I said yes, which I'm not going to, how would we create a life together?"

"I don't know. Asking you to move far away from your family is bad enough, but leaving your job... I hadn't counted on that being a problem. I'll need to do more thinking." He reached for her hand.

She almost pulled it out of reach, but then... she didn't. She loved touching him, being touched by him.

He wove his fingers through hers. "I went about this all wrong."

"You think?"

"Making love to you was like a religious experience. I even said a little prayer at the end, giving thanks for what we'd shared."

That touched her. She didn't want to go all mushy inside, but he had a way about him. She'd wanted to hug him from the moment he'd taken the postcard out of his shirt pocket.

He squeezed her hand and looked at her. "You can probably guess I've never proposed to anyone before, judging from the arseways I handled it."

"It wasn't what you'd call smooth."

"Or respectful. It was more of a demand than a request."

"If you're working up to a do-over, it's not a good idea. I'll just shoot you down."

He nodded. "Any sane person would. My plan is banjaxed. But let's say that a miracle happened, and a path opened that would allow us to be together without me leaving granny to fend for herself or you giving up your job."

"That would take a big miracle."

"But pretend that happened. Could you see yourself marrying me?"

"After knowing you for less than a day?"

"Good point. I've known you for years, wanted you for years." He flashed her his winning smile. "I don't suppose I look like your dream fella."

"I don't have one. But... I like the way you look. I like it a lot."

"So you approve of my looks and you enjoyed the sex. There was also that moment when we took a walk with Sam and you said some nice things about me."

"Now you're fishing."

"Have to. I need all the arguments I can find. I remember something about *pure gold*. Did you mean that?"

He was utterly sincere and completely adorable. "Are you sure you're a construction worker? Because you're sounding more and more like a lawyer."

"I have to say, *pure gold* sounds like the sort of thing you'd look for in a partner."

"All right." She couldn't keep her smile from breaking through. "You've impressed me from the get-go. But I would never agree to marry someone, even hypothetically, when I've only spent a few hours with him."

"Very intense hours. We've had a chance to show our true colors. We've had quality over quantity. We—"

"Give it a rest, counselor."

"Meaning?"

"You won't get an answer from me tonight." She let the sheet fall away. "But if you're willing to drop the subject, you might get something else."

21

That hadn't gone as bad as it could have. And Kieran made sure the rest of the evening was a roaring success. He loved the hell out of Sara until they were both too exhausted to do more than kiss goodnight and curl up together in Rance's king-sized bed.

The alarm they'd set chimed at four-fifteen. They both staggered out of bed and bumped into each other as they sorted through the clothes on the floor.

"We need to be more organized next time," Sara mumbled.

"Next time?" The cobwebs disappeared from his brain. "You'll come back again?"

"At the risk of adding ammunition to your argument, I'll admit that I've never had sex this good and I want more of it."

"If you think I'm too sleepy to remember that, I'm not." He'd cherish that comment for the rest of his days.

"Speaking of sleep, why are you getting dressed? You don't have to go anywhere. You can just stay here and catch up. I'll bet you're still jet-lagged."

"I'm walking you out to the porch. That's what we pure gold fellas do."

"Until you pass out from lack of sleep. You need to conserve your energy. Aren't you and Lucky doing a nine o'clock call to your granny?"

"We are."

"Are you going to say anything about me?"

"I don't know. I could, since Lucky's in on this secret."

"Do you want my opinion?"

"I do, yeah."

"Don't say anything about me. You'll be giving her enough emotional news about your mom and Lucky. Even Oksana won't be on the call. Mentioning me, even if you only refer to me as a new friend, could add confusion."

"That's good advice. I'll take it. But I'll need to tell her about you eventually. Just so you know, she'd believe I've found my dream girl and it was meant to be."

"Which could only make the situation more difficult for both of you."

"Maybe." His gut tightened. No maybe about it.

"I hear Rance's truck." She picked up her jacket and put it on. "I just need my phone. Where—"

"Here." He took it off the bedside table, handed it to her and followed her into the living room. He didn't want her to leave. "I'll text you after the phone call with Granny. I don't know what the schedule is apart from that."

"Me, either."

"But I'll see you. At lunch, or dinner, or—"

"We'll see each other." She turned and gave him a quick kiss. "Good luck with the call."

"Thanks." He opened the door and cold air blew in.

"Stay in the cabin. Go back to bed."

"No, ma'am." He stepped out on the porch in his bare feet. He hadn't bothered to locate his socks so he could put on his boots.

She turned back one more time. "See you soon."

"Very soon." But not soon enough.

Rance stood in front of Midnight Thunder, arms crossed, probably because it was bleedin' cold outside at this hour. Rance had a short conversation with Sara. Then he helped her into the driver's side and did something with the seat again.

That lass had gumption, but if she was as knackered as he was... well, he had to trust her judgment, didn't he?

She backed around nice and easy as if she owned that vehicle. Then she drove away.

Like an eejit, he stood shivering until the forest blocked the red taillights. He'd made a mess out of proposing to her, no question. But he didn't regret doing it.

If he'd stopped to think, he wouldn't have said those two words. They'd still be locked away, maybe forever.

But now she knew his heart, even if she thought he was off his rocker. She liked him, even admired him. She loved the sex and his accent. He could build on that.

Getting her to love him enough to want to marry him wouldn't be hard. Finding a way to be together once she loved him — there was the challenge. Before he tackled that one, he needed more sleep.

Returning to the bedroom, he shucked his clothes and laid down on the sheets that smelled of sex. The heady aroma reminded him that she'd be back. Smiling, he pulled up the covers and closed his eyes.

A sharp rapping on the open bedroom door roused him from the deepest sleep he'd had in years. Sunlight filled the room.

"Time to get up, buddy," Rance called out from the doorway. "You're due at the house in an hour for that phone call with Lucky."

"Thanks." He cleared his throat. "Thank you." What would he do without that fella?

He grabbed a quick shower and shave before pulling clothes out of his duffel. A wee bit wrinkled, but they'd have to do. The scent of coffee drew him to the kitchen.

Rance stood at the stove. "Don't know what you usually have for breakfast, but I'm making us each a fried egg sandwich. We can eat fast."

"That would be grand." He'd read enough about Montana to know black pudding wouldn't likely be on the menu around here. "I appreciate it."

"I talked to Lucky and he'd actually like you there early so the two of you can work out how you'll break the news."

"That would be smart, now, wouldn't it?" Preplanning an important conversation. What a concept. "Can I help with anything?"

"It's done. Just get yourself some coffee." He carried two plates to a small round kitchen table.

"You're taking good care of me, mate." He poured a mug of coffee and joined Rance at the table.

"Glad to. How'd it go? I mean, generally. I'm not asking for details." He bit into his sandwich.

"We enjoyed ourselves."

Nodding in approval, he swallowed. "Just what I hoped for."

"I asked her to marry me."

"Sure you did." Rance flashed him a grin. Then he paused, his eyes growing wide. "You're not kidding."

"I'm not. She didn't tell you?" That pleased him.

"She did *not* tell me. What the hell, dude? Are you nuts?"

"That's what she thinks. Speaking of planning what to say in advance, I sure didn't plan to say that. It just came out. At least she has something to think about."

"That's for damned sure." His look of shock had changed to fascination. "I have to give it you, though. You've got solid brass ones, buddy."

He shrugged. "It was like I couldn't stop myself from saying it."

"You obviously didn't run her off. She wants to come back tonight and drive over alone, like I originally planned."

"That'd be easier on you."

"Yeah, and she's taken to that truck like I thought she would. But if her sister says no, I'll ride with her. Don't want to tick off Lani when she's starting to thaw."

"How do you know?"

"Talked with her last night."

"Oh, did you, now? I thought you weren't gonna—"

"I didn't. We didn't. I can tell she wants me but she doesn't want to want me."

"In other words, she doesn't like you."

"Sometimes she does. I can make her laugh, but that's part of the problem. She thinks that everything's a joke to me. That I have no depth, no ambition to be anything except a bartender."

"Is she right?"

"A couple of years ago, she would've been. Not now. But she's heard all the stories about me and drawn her conclusions."

"What about this story? You're going to a lot of trouble for Sara and me. You're not treating that like a joke."

"Yeah, but she's suspicious. For good reason, I might add." He picked up his phone from the table and checked the time. "Drink your coffee and I'll wrap the rest of our sandwiches in a napkin so we can eat 'em on the way. I promised Lucky I'd get you there early."

And Rance was a man of his word. Kieran valued that quality and so far he'd found it in abundance when dealing with the McLintocks.

On the drive back to the house, Rance educated him on the trees they passed. Most were evergreens, something he didn't see much of in the farmland surrounding his village. This heavily forested landscape couldn't be more different from the tidy fields of County Kildare.

His young, restless mother must have yearned for something more, a wild and unpredictable place. Snow-capped mountains and dense stands of tall trees would certainly qualify. If she'd had her way, he would have shared in her adventure, for better or worse.

He'd made this trip to solve the mystery of her disappearance, or so he'd told himself. But surrounded by this magnificent landscape, he'd gained something he hadn't admitted he was after — understanding. Now he could forgive her.

He wouldn't say that to Granny today, though. He might never say it. He'd had to walk in his mother's shoes to gain that understanding. Granny had no wish to do that.

22

"You have to get up or Mom and Dad will think you're sick. We're supposed to leave for the Missoula shopping trip around nine-thirty."

Sara reluctantly opened her eyes. A glass of orange juice was inches from her nose. "What time is it?"

"Ten minutes to nine. According to their calculations, you've been asleep for almost twelve hours. That's not normal."

"I'll get up. Move the orange juice."

The juice shifted away and she sat up. "I'll have you know I was sound asleep."

"I'm aware. Just be glad it's me in here and not Mom with a thermometer. Drink this."

"Yes, mommy dearest."

"Smartass. FYI, I covered for you by saying we stayed up late talking. You're welcome."

"Thanks, but then why didn't you sleep in, too?" She took the juice and guzzled it. She was thirstier than she realized.

"Because I never do, remember?" Lani plopped down on the other bed. "Doesn't matter how long I stay up, I'm out of bed at my regular time." She didn't sound particularly happy about it.

"It's because you're anal. I'd forgotten that now that we don't live in the same house." She put down the empty glass. "Are you bummed that they're selling it?"

"Kind of. I have some savings. I might be able to swing a home loan."

"You'd buy it?"

"I don't know. It's not like I need a three-bedroom house in the suburbs. Anyway, I have time to think about it since it's not on the market yet." She took back the glass. "So, how was it? Not that I need to ask. He clearly wore you out."

"It was perfect, except for one thing."

"He snores."

"No. At least I don't think so. I conked out." And maybe she wouldn't tell Lani about the proposal. "It's a wonder I heard the alarm."

"I'm glad you did. I heard Rance's go off at four and almost felt sorry for the guy. But he did it to himself."

And Lani had conveniently switched topics. "Rance has been awesome. He offered to let me drive over, and I *loved* it. I drove back here this morning, too. I can handle Thunder just fine and I know the way, now. I want to save him those extra trips."

"Did you tell him that?"

"I said I'd ask you, and he said you're the boss."

Her sister's lips twitched like she was trying not to smile.

"I'm totally safe and I'll have my phone."

"Okay. Now that you're checked out on it, I'm not so worried."

"I'm telling you, it's a blast. You sit up so high, like you're queen of the world and your chariot is at your command, ready to take you wherever you want. Driving Thunder's a power trip. You should ask him if he'll let you—"

"No, thanks." Lani rolled her eyes. "But I can see why that truck appeals to him."

Sara opened her mouth to defend Rance's choice of vehicle but changed her mind. "Yeah, now that I think about it, Thunder's not your style."

"Nope, but if you're happy driving it, that simplifies things."

"Sure does."

"What kept last night from being perfect?"

Damn, she'd circled back. Time to minimize the event. "I'm going to blame it on jetlag. And maybe being Irish. They seem to be an emotional bunch. "

"What did he do?"

"He proposed, but I'm sure—"

"*No!*" Lani clapped a hand over her mouth and glanced toward the closed door as if someone might charge through it because of her outburst.

"Probably just a knee-jerk reaction. The first time was incredible for both of us. That's unusual. He said the words just popped out, and I believe him."

"But did he take it back?"

"No, he doubled down. Maybe he felt he had to, like once he'd committed, he had to stick to his guns. When I said it wasn't even a remote possibility and we should just drop the subject, he did." She was fudging a little. He'd asked whether she'd consider marrying him if all the obstacles were removed. She'd refused to answer him, but the question was still very much on the table.

"Then you think it was a mistake and he didn't know how to back out of making the offer?"

"Possibly." But in her heart she knew it was no mistake. A miscalculation, for sure, but the fire in his blue eyes when he'd said *marry me* had been real. Thrillingly real. The words had ignited an irrational response in her passion-drenched body. She'd almost said yes.

23

Lucky had chosen Rowdy Roost as the best spot for making the phone call, which suited Kieran fine. He had good memories of the place — his dart game with Lucky and dancing with Sara.

He hadn't heard from her but hadn't expected to. She might still be asleep. He would be, too, if his host hadn't made sure he didn't miss this critical appointment with Lucky.

Rance parked by the side doors and they both climbed out. Lucky was already inside working on his pool game judging from the sound of balls smacking against each other.

"I didn't get that lesson, did I, mate?"

"No worries." Rance opened the door and ushered him inside. "Get Lucky to give you a lesson." He raised his voice. "He's almost as good as I am."

Lucky straightened, pool cue in hand. "Pay no attention to him, Kieran. He thinks I can't beat him anymore now that he has his own table."

"I don't just think, bro. It's a fact. Last time we played—"

"I was rusty. I'll admit it. But unlike you, Oksana and I have our evenings free. She does writing sprints with Mom and I work on my game."

"Then I look forward to our next match. Either of you want coffee?"

Kieran shook his head. "No, thanks."

"None for me, either," Lucky said. "I'm wired enough as it is."

"Then I'll leave you to it." He paused next to Lucky. "You're gonna make that lady's day."

"Hope so. She's definitely gonna make mine."

Rance lifted his hand and Lucky grasped it as they exchanged a glance of solidarity gained through a shared life in the family trenches.

Kieran's throat tightened. He had mates he'd known for years, but it wasn't the same.

Rance left and Lucky snapped his cue back into its holder on the wall. "Did last night work out?"

"It did." He would have revealed more. After all, this was his brother, even if they hadn't spent years together. But now wasn't the time.

"Glad to hear it." Lucky distributed the balls among the table's pockets and stepped away. "I'm thinking you'll want to tell her about our mom first, and I'll just sit quietly and listen to that part."

"That makes sense." He pulled out his mobile. "Her story leads right into the part of you coming into the world. At that point, I'll hand it over to you. You can tell her about yourself."

"What sort of stuff should I tell her?"

"Don't worry. She'll ask questions. Where should we sit?"

"I like the bar."

"Me, too." He followed Lucky and took the stool next to his. "I texted her on the way over and told her I'd call at four her time."

"Did she answer?"

"She did. I want to show you the way she texts. It's gas."

"Meaning funny, right?"

He nodded as he called up the thread. "She loves emojis but they hardly ever match what she's texting. She pretends she doesn't need her glasses, and even when she knows she tapped the wrong thing, she won't use the delete button. She's afraid it'll all disappear."

"Which, to be fair, can happen if you hold it down too long."

"I think she did that once, lost a long message and had to start over. She's never touched that button again." He handed over his mobile. "That's the most recent. The one that starts *I'LL BE HERE.*"

"Does she always use caps?"

"Only when she's in a hurry."

"The rose is nice, and the hearts."

"I personally like the hammer paired with the T-rex."

Lucky grinned. "If I met a T-rex, I wouldn't mind having a hammer."

"Scroll up and you'll see the ones she sent earlier."

He started reading and chuckled. "She's clearly worried about you getting enough food. The volcano's an interesting choice. And the barber's pole. Hey, she found a bowl of ice cream. That works."

"And a tooth. I think that counts."

Peering closer, Lucky's grin widened. "Technically, so does a pile of poo."

"Don't *ever* tell her she sent that, mate. I'm sure she doesn't know what it is. She'd be scarlet."

"I promise." Still smiling, he handed back the mobile. "I love her already. Would she text me some emojis if I give her my number?"

"I'm sure she'd want to, but you'll have to text her first and then she can just reply. Once I get home I'll put you in her contacts with your picture. She'll love that. Right now I'm the only contact she has."

"Got it."

"It's time." Pulling up his contacts, he tapped on Granny's listing and set his mobile on speaker mode.

She answered right away, breathless with excitement. "Ah, Kieran, my boy, I miss ya so!"

"I miss you, too, oul dear. And I have news about my mother."

"Do ya?" Her voice trembled. "She's gone, yeah?"

"She is." He said it gently. "Not long after she mailed that postcard, but—"

"I knew it, knew it in my bones." She sniffed. "Sorry, sorry. I'll be after a tissue. Be right back."

His chest ached. If only he could be there.

"It's back, I am." Her voice was stronger. "So. My Freya is gone from this world. But d'ya know where she is?"

"I'm sure she's in heaven, Granny. I know she had her faults, but—"

"I don't mean that. A'course she's in heaven. And if she's not, she's down there givin' the Devil what for. I meant, d'ya know..." Her voice faltered. "Where is she... I hope someone...."

"Oh." He sucked in a breath. "She's in the Wagon Train cemetery. She had a proper burial." He looked over at Lucky. "And a headstone with... her name on it."

"Truly? You've seen it?"

"Not yet. I'll go there today."

"And you'll send me a picture?"

"I will." Why had he promised to do that today? The headstone would still be wrong. Well, he'd figure out something.

"How'd... how'd it happen?"

"She died in childbirth, Granny."

She gasped. "A wee baby? Oh, no! Did they both—"

"The baby lived, and—"

"*Lived*? Are you sayin' I have a *grandchild* there?" And now she was crying.

So was he. Tears dribbled down his cheeks. He didn't dare look at Lucky in case he was in the same condition. He cleared his throat. "You do. And—"

"Holy Mother of God." She continued to weep. "A grandchild. All this time. Freya gave me another grandchild. I can't believe it."

He did his best to hold it together for her sake and Lucky's. "A grand*son*. You have a grandson. And I have a—" He swallowed. "He's right here. I'll let you—" He passed the mobile to his half-brother, who was mopping his face with a bandana. He grabbed a napkin from a holder on the bar.

Shoving the bandana in his back pocket, Lucky sniffed and dragged in a breath. "Hi, Granny." His chest heaved. "I'm your grandson. I'm Lucky."

"Oh, my boy," she choked out between sobs, "'Tis not *luck* you're havin'. You're a fecking miracle!"

24

Sara excused herself from the shopping trip by saying she needed to wash her hair and she didn't want to hold them up. Her parents would have waited, but Lani came up with a logical reason to leave ASAP, something to do with traffic.

Good old Lani must have figured out that she wanted to stick around to see Kieran and ask how the nine o'clock phone call with his granny and Lucky had gone. Her sister was coming through like a champ.

Sara already had Lani's birthday present, which she'd tucked out of sight in a pocket of her suitcase. Lucky and Oksana had located an out-of-print copy of a book Lani had wanted for years.

But she deserved something extra for her kindness and support regarding Kieran. Sara didn't know what that extra thing would be, but she had until the party on Saturday to brainstorm.

She took a shower and also washed her hair so she wouldn't be a liar. Washing it wasn't a bad idea since she'd be seeing Kieran again tonight, but she didn't linger in the shower because she was starving.

Anxiety about the rendezvous plan had kept her from eating much at dinner last night. Although her sexual adventure with Kieran had started out sweet and slow, after their talk it had become gloriously physical. She'd worked up an appetite.

Venturing into the kitchen, she found Rance at the small table tucked into a corner of the spacious room.

He put down his coffee and looked up from a copy of *The Sentinel*, Wagon Train's weekly newspaper. He had a small plate in front of him with nothing on it but a few crumbs. "Hey, there. What're you up to?"

"Same as you, hanging around waiting to find out how the call went. Have you heard anything?"

"Far as I know, they're still in Rowdy Roost talking to her. Not surprising. That lady looks like she'd be loaded with questions."

"You took a shine to her, didn't you?"

"Damn straight. Like I said, this crew is short on grandmas, and I'm talking about the ones in her age bracket, not Marybeth's, who's almost too young to qualify for our bunch."

"But she treats you like a grandma would."

"Sort of, but she's harder on us than the grandma I have in my head." He peered at her. "I just happened to think. Do you have one you can donate to the cause?"

"Not really. My dad's folks had him late and they're both gone. Mom's parents moved to Florida a few years ago and there's no way they'd give up their beach house to live in snow country again."

"Bummer."

"Listen, I hate to be a PITA and mess up the kitchen, but I'm really hungry. Who should I ask about fixing myself something?"

"You're looking at him."

"But you don't live here."

"Doesn't sleeping here count?"

"Shh. Don't say that so loud."

"Don't worry. Nobody's around. Mom's in her office writing and Sam's in there napping. Andy's down at the *Sentinel*, also writing. Marybeth's off on some errand in town. It's just you and me, kid. And those two jokers in Rowdy Roost." He stood. "What are you hungry for?"

"Anything."

"French toast?"

"Oh, God, that sounds wonderful but not exactly healthy. What did you have on that plate?"

"A cinnamon roll."

"Mmm."

"Last one. Sorry. C'mon. Have some French toast. I'll help you make it."

"Who's having French toast?" Lucky walked into the kitchen, followed by Kieran. "I want in." He glanced over his shoulder. "How about you, bro?"

Bro. Sara's breath caught. The McLintocks used that term for each other, but this was the first time she'd heard Lucky address Kieran that way. Maybe it was her imagination, but she'd swear Kieran reacted like she had, with a quick intake of breath.

His gaze sought hers briefly. He gave her a quick smile before looking away. "I'd love some

French toast. I'll help make it. Granny and I have it all the time back home."

Lucky and Rance set up an assembly line with her cracking eggs, Kieran mixing, Rance dipping and Lucky frying. She and Kieran were finished first.

"Sara," Lucky called out. "You're in charge of plates and silverware since you know where everything is. Kieran, toppings are in the fridge."

He opened the door. "What qualifies as a topping?"

"Anything you want," Rance said as he made a fresh pot of coffee. "No rules."

Kieran chuckled. "I like it."

Happiness flooded through her. Kieran had never experienced the joy of having siblings. His relaxed smile and the sparkle in his eyes said more than words that he was enjoying the hell out of it.

Nobody had brought up the phone call, not even after the four of them were seated at the small kitchen table, elbows almost touching as they dived into their feast. Sara vowed not to be the first one to ask about it. She was counting on Rance.

He did not disappoint. "Hey, show a little mercy, you two. Sara and I are dying to hear about the phone call. Must have been a long one."

Lucky glanced at Kieran. "Not so long. We hung up about twenty minutes ago. We needed...."

"The truth is, we bawled like babies on that call." Kieran's cheeks turned pink. "We needed to pull ourselves together. Good thing nobody was there but Lucky and me."

"A very good thing. And then, when I said *I'm Lucky*, she thought I was being disrespectful. It wasn't *luck*, it was the hand of God, and I shouldn't imply otherwise."

Sara couldn't help smiling. "I'll bet that's not the only time your name's caused you trouble."

"No, but she's my most stubborn case so far. I couldn't convince her it was my name, not my opinion. She finally believed me when I told her I was born on March 17th."

"By that time we were laughing *and* crying." Kieran shook his head. "It was a holy show."

"But good." Lucky grinned. "Very good. In the end, she was happy about my name and my birthday. She's a riot. I can't wait to meet her in person."

Rance jumped on that. "She's coming over?"

"No. I promised I'd go over there."

"Did you ask her to come?"

Lucky exchanged another glance with Kieran. "You know, after talking with her, I think Kieran's right. A trip to Rowdy Ranch could be hard on her. I was afraid even asking her to come would stress her out. So I didn't."

Rance sighed. "Yeah, okay. I can see how bringing that up when she's still adjusting to the idea that you exist would be bad timing. She also needs more info about this place."

"Oh, she wants pictures," Kieran said. "I'll text her some today. And she asked if Desiree could please be on the call tomorrow, so she can thank her. She's writing her a letter right this minute, but she wants to talk to her, too."

"Mom will love talking to her." Lucky pushed back his empty plate. "She usually starts writing by nine but since her deadline isn't looming, I'll bet she'll make the time tomorrow. I'll advise her to bring tissues, though."

"I also told Granny I'd take a picture of the grave." Kieran looked at Rance and Sara. "Do either of you know what's happening with the headstone?"

"I don't," Rance said.

"Desiree has more information." Sara hesitated. Was she the one who should be telling him about it, though?

"Like what?"

"Fixing it won't be as easy as she thought."

"Then it might not get done before I leave?"

"Maybe not." Definitely not, but that wasn't her news to tell.

"Well, then." Lucky glanced around the group. "Kieran said he'd send her a picture today, so what should we—"

"I'll text her and say it'll be another day. I shouldn't have said that I'd—"

"We need to fake it." Rance put down his coffee mug. "I had a feeling this could be an issue. It's a picture. Everybody alters pictures these days. Surely someone in this family can handle that."

"Molly," Lucky said. "With all the PR she's doing for Mrs. J's B&B, she'll have a photo editing program on her computer." He stood. "Let's clean up the dishes and then Kieran and I will go out to the cemetery and take the picture."

Sara got up and grabbed her plate and mug. "You need flowers."

"You can add those digitally, too," Rance said.

"We'll not be adding them digitally." Kieran held Lucky's gaze. "Right?"

"Absolutely. We'll stop by the Wagon Train Market on the way."

"I'd tag along," Rance said, "but I'm due at the Buffalo."

"Can I please go?" Inviting herself was cheeky, but she wanted to be there.

Kieran's warm glance confirmed it was the right thing to do. "I was hoping you would, lass."

25

Walking into the kitchen and finding Sara there had been the gift Kieran had hoped for. Lucky had told him a shopping trip to Missoula was on her family's agenda. Sara had stayed back. For him. He had no doubt of that.

"I have an idea," Lucky said once they'd piled into his truck, Sara in the front passenger seat and Kieran in the back. "We'll be going into town, and if you have the keys to your rental—"

"In my pocket. I brought them today in case someone could take me in so I could drive that vehicle out to the ranch."

"If you do that after we visit the cemetery you can take Sara back and I'll head over to the bookshop."

"I wouldn't mind seeing that shop today."

Lucky grinned. "And I wouldn't mind showing it to you."

"It's cozy." Sara swiveled in her seat and glanced back at him. "You'll like it."

"I know I will. I'll buy my first M.R. Morrison book today."

Lucky glanced at him in the rearview mirror. "She'd be happy to give you one."

"I know she would, but I'd rather buy one from you, mate. No, wait. I'll buy two, one for me and one for Granny."

"She reads Westerns?"

"She doesn't read much fiction, let alone Westerns. She's into biographies, mostly. But I think she'd read one of Desiree's if it comes from your shop and I have your mom sign it. Even if she doesn't read it, she'll love having it on display to show the neighbors."

"Then I'll give you the one for Granny. How's that?"

"But—"

"I want to send something back with you, bro, and a book would be perfect. I'll let you pay for yours, but hers will be my gift to her."

"Can't argue with that. She'll be thrilled." And didn't he love it when Lucky called him *bro*? He hadn't felt natural doing the same, but before he left he'd try it out.

At the market they each bought a bouquet, looking for the ones in non-breakable containers. Their drive to the cemetery was silent.

Lucky finally spoke as he pulled into the parking lot of the white clapboard country church. The graveyard was off to the left, bordered by a black wrought-iron fence. "I said I hadn't been to the grave much, but the truth is, I've only been once, the day I asked to see where my birth mother was buried. I was five. Haven't been back since."

Sara reached over and touched his arm. "She didn't let herself be known. It's hard to care when a person is nothing but a shadow."

"Sara's right." Kieran unfastened his seat belt and leaned forward. "Don't blame yourself, boyo. I'm just now forgiving her. I came over here mad as hell."

"I was mad, too. If Mom hadn't been in that hospital having Rance, I'd have been SOL."

"You need to come to County Kildare. It's grand for most people living there, including Granny. But it didn't suit Freya. She had too much fire in her."

Lucky nodded. "I will come." He glanced over his shoulder. "Does County Kildare suit you?"

"You ask hard questions."

He grimaced. "So I've been told. Never mind."

"Let's just say it suits me well enough. Granny devoted her life to raising me when all her friends were long past that stage. I'll never forget that."

"Understood." Lucky opened his door. "Let's pay a visit to Freya Noreen Haggerty."

"Do you remember where she is?" He and Sara followed Lucky through the gate.

"Oh, yeah. I was the smartest five-year-old you'll ever meet."

"Wow, good for you." Sara switched her bouquet to her other hand and adjusted the strap of her shoulder purse as she picked her way along the gravel path. "You must have a photographic memory."

"No, just a degree in smartassery. I don't remember. I asked Mom for directions."

"She comes out here?" Kieran hadn't expected that.

"Much to my surprise, she does. I figured we'd be coming eventually so I got to the house this morning before she started working to get info. I thought she'd have to look it up. She told me exactly where to go."

"How often does she come? Did she say?"

"Every year the day after Rance's and my birthday. She checks on the condition of the gravesite and gives thanks for… for me."

The last part sounded suspiciously husky.

"And here we are." Lucky paused in front of a grave covered with neatly trimmed grass.

The modest headstone contained all the information Desiree had possessed, a name and a date.

Kieran waited for sadness to come, or relief, or closure. Nothing. He glanced at Lucky. "I was pure dreading this. But…"

"It's weird. You'd think now that I know more, I'd feel a connection. But I don't."

"Having the wrong name doesn't help." Sara gazed at the headstone. 'It might be different if you had everything on there — Freya Noreen Haggerty and her date of birth as well as her date of death. How old was she?"

"Twenty-two. Granny celebrates it every June 13th."

"I'll make sure Molly gets that info." Lucky held his bouquet in the crook of his arm as he pulled out his mobile and tapped on it. "We should take our picture and send it. Molly needs time to work her magic." He set his bouquet by the headstone.

Sara put hers next to it and then Kieran added his. The bright flowers lined up at the base of the granite slab helped. Lucky tapped on his mobile and backed up, moving to the foot of the grave.

"Wait." Sara took her mobile out of her purse. "You two should be in it."

"Should we?" Kieran glanced at Lucky.

He shrugged. "It's for Granny. It shows that we were here together. It's our mother's grave. Why not?"

"On either side, then?" He looked to Sara for direction.

"One of you on each side and take off your hats."

"Yes, ma'am." He removed his Stetson and finger-combed his hair.

Putting away his mobile, Lucky did the same. "Should we smile? I don't think we should smile."

"But then we'll look like we don't give a feck."

Lucky snorted. "Sorry. This is not a laughing matter."

"Or maybe it is, mate. We're hoping to fool an oul dear into thinking this banjaxed headstone is fine and dandy. That's a story you tell in the pub over a couple of pints."

Lucky flashed him a grin. "Hadn't thought of it that way."

"Here's an idea." Sara took another step back. "Look at each other instead of at the camera. And smile just a little bit."

Kieran turned slightly so he could see Lucky. The fella was wearing the goofiest fake smile ever. "What is that?"

"My half smile." He said it while trying to keep his lips in position.

"It needs work."

That set Lucky off and once he started laughing, Kieran couldn't help himself. When he finally regained control, he looked around to see if anyone was in the cemetery apart from the three of them.

"Nobody else is here," Lucky said. "I figured it would be deserted on a weekday morning."

"Are you two eejits ready to try it again?"

Keiran gave Sara a thumbs-up. "Well spoken, lass." He checked with Lucky. "Don't do the half-smile."

"Should we shake hands, instead?"

"Like we're concluding a business deal? I think not. Let's just look at each other."

"Okay." Lucky's eyes twinkled. "For the record, I give a feck."

"Yeah, me, too."

"Okay!" Sara called out. "I took several. Good job."

Putting on his hat, Kieran looked down at the grave. "She did give us life."

"So true." Lucky's gaze dropped. "And a good hair color. I'm glad I got hers, especially now that I know the scumbag she ran off with was blond."

"My gobshite father was blond, too. She had a type."

"I liked hearing she was a reader, though." His voice softened. "Granny seemed proud of that."

"She is." Leaning down, he shifted the pots so they were lined up better. "Mum was a fine student."

"I thought my love of books was all my mom, but maybe some was her doing." Crouching, he plucked a small weed and tossed it aside. Then he gently laid his palm on the grassy mound.

Kieran's breath hitched. Seeing Lucky do that got to him. His brother had never felt her arms around him, but he had. A warm hug, the scent of her perfume... the memory hovered... and was gone.

When Lucky straightened, he blinked away a sheen of moisture. "Thank God she sent that last postcard." He swallowed. "What you did, using your life savings to come over here...." His chest heaved. "I won't ever be able to thank you enough."

Kieran looked right back, memorizing Lucky's face. Emotions crowded his chest and clogged his throat. "I think you just did, bro."

<u>26</u>

Sara had captured it all. She'd decided to leave her Stetson at home today but she loved that Kieran had made sure to wear his. No one would doubt those two guys were related.

She had their laughing fit on video and stills of all the other precious moments. The emotions they couldn't find when they'd first arrived at this gravesite had finally spilled out of them, the sorrow, the laughter, the love.

No telling how they'd react to her paparazzi behavior. They'd had no idea the cameras were rolling. She'd keep the extra pictures and video to herself for now. If they didn't want them, she did.

She'd grabbed those images without hesitation, desperate to save something of Kieran. Losing him completely at the end of the week was unthinkable. No point in denying it. She loved him.

When they moved away from the headstone and walked toward her, she quickly scrolled to the three shots most likely to work for the project. They approved her choices. Then Lucky gave her his number and she transferred the pictures to his phone.

Their exit from the graveyard was much faster and more cheerful than their entrance. They paused in the parking lot while Lucky sent the images to Molly along with an explanation.

The trip to L'Amour and More took all of three minutes. Sara offered to be the official photographer inside the bookshop, too. She had a ready excuse — Kieran was free to interact with Lucky and Oksana while they proudly showed off their beloved shop.

Whenever a candid shot turned out especially well, she texted it to his phone. He'd have plenty of images to choose from the next time he sent Granny pictures.

When Oksana suggested getting some shots of Sara with Kieran, she nixed the idea. Better not to have any evidence that his granny might see. She'd have questions and they had no answers.

After Kieran had explored the bookshop and chosen two hardback copies of Desiree's first book to take home, he was ready to tackle the drive to the ranch. They walked the short distance to Hannigan's, where his small white sedan sat right where he'd left it.

He glanced at the entrance to Hannigan's. "Should I see if Justine's there and tell her the news?"

"Do you want to?"

"I do, but not now." He pulled the keys out of his pocket. "I'd rather get this drive over with."

"Let's do it."

"Then in you go." He opened the driver's side door.

She glanced at him in confusion. Was he hoping she'd take the wheel? "Sorry, but I can't. It would be against your rental agreement for me to drive."

"I wasn't asking you—" He looked inside the car. "Oh."

"Ah. You thought that was the passenger side."

He gave her a sheepish grin. "I did, yeah. Let's try this again. Come with me." Leaving the door open, he walked around the back of the car and opened the front passenger door with a flourish. "In you go."

"Thanks." She slid onto the warm seat. The interior had been spritzed with something to make it smell better. She didn't agree with the choice.

Climbing behind the wheel, he laid his hat on the dash. "Scundered again." He shut the door, which made the smell more pronounced.

"Which means?"

"I embarrassed myself."

"Hey, I promise you I'd do the same thing in Ireland."

He looked at her and grinned. "Thanks for saying that. And you would. One of my mates works at a car rental and the stories he tells are gas." He latched his seatbelt. "I was just trying to impress you with my cowboy manners. These McLintock fellas could teach me a thing or two."

"I happen to think you're fine the way you are."

He looked at her, a question lurking in his eyes. "Is that so?"

"Last night you asked whether I'd consider you if the problems magically disappeared."

His gaze sharpened. "I did ask that, yeah."

"I would."

His face relaxed into a beautiful smile. "I knew it!"

"You did not!"

"You gave yourself away, lass, taking all those extra pictures at the cemetery. Even a video."

Caught. She flushed. "How'd you—"

"Lethal sharp hearing." He leaned closer and cupped her cheek. "I'm honored that you feel the same about me as I feel about you."

His tender gaze created a sweet ache, a longing to be held, to be loved. "It's hopeless, you know."

"Let's not tell ourselves that." He brushed his thumb over her cheek.

"But realistically—"

"Let's be unrealistic."

"That will only—"

"Make it worse at the end? Then don't think about the end. If I could kiss you right now, you'd stop thinking and start feeling, but it's not the place. And this car stinks."

That made her smile. "It does."

"Fancy putting down the windows on the way back?"

"I do."

"Then let's get out of here." Facing forward, he switched on the engine, studied the buttons on the armrest and put down the windows. "Ahhh, better. I was afraid to do that yesterday, when I was up to ninety with massive vehicles on all sides."

"You were going ninety?"

"Not really. It's just what we say. I kept the needle around seventy-five." Checking his mirrors, he put the car in reverse and backed out. "Also I didn't know which button. I could hit the wrong one while I was tearing down the motorway and make my seat tilt backwards."

"Sounds like you've seen *Planes, Trains and Automobiles*."

"That I have." He chuckled. "Took off my jacket before I got in because of that film." He headed down Main Street.

"Do you know the route? Or do you need me to—"

"I'm fine. I paid attention when we drove to the ranch yesterday and came back to town today. I still have the urge to go on the left, though."

"I wouldn't advise it."

"What's the limit in town?"

"Twenty-five." She stayed quiet as he navigated his way to the two-lane that would take them out to Rowdy Ranch. "The limit on this road is seventy in the daytime and sixty-five at night."

He increased his speed to forty-five. "If I do seventy, you'll be blown to bits."

"But if we put up the windows we'll be stuck with the smell."

"I'll keep it at forty-five for now and let this fella go ahead of us." Thrusting his arm out the window, he waved the truck around. As it roared past, he glanced in the rearview mirror. "That's it for now. Not much traffic on this road."

"The McLintocks hope it'll stay that way. As word gets out about M.R. Morrison, they want to keep the ranch's location a secret."

"Think they will?"

"It could be a challenge. Stephen King fans are wild to see his house and the iconic locations in Bangor, Maine. Those tours are always fully booked. I think Desiree's a little worried about maintaining the family's privacy."

"Speaking of privacy...." He glanced over at her. "Have you copped to the opportunity we've been given?"

"You mean being alone in this car?"

"It's more than that."

"Hang on, mister. I like you a lot, but not enough to have back-seat sex in the boonies in the middle of the day."

"We don't need a back seat. Rance is at work."

It took a second, but then she sucked in a breath and glanced at him. "I totally missed that."

"Not only is he at work, so is everybody else."

Her body began to tingle. "And my family's in Missoula. We're left to our own devices."

"So we are."

"Is that the real reason you didn't want to go talk to Justine?"

He laughed. "It was, yeah."

"Then why are you poking along at forty-five?"

"Didn't want to blow you to bits."

"Can I borrow your hat?"

"Sure."

Scooping her hair into a high ponytail, she flipped it on top of her head and crammed on his hat. "Pedal to the metal, cowboy!"

With a whoop, he stomped on the gas and the little sedan shot forward.

She kept her hand on his precious hat so it wouldn't fly out the window as they raced down the highway. Although she avoided looking at the speedometer, she kept an eye out for Smoky. "You'll need to go way slower on the ranch road!" she called out over the rush of air through the open windows.

"Understood!" He flashed her a grin.

Oh, yeah, she loved this Irishman. She could hardly wait for him to take her in his arms. He'd promised to help her escape reality. And he was a man of his word.

27

Hurtling down the road at speeds he never drove at home, Kieran surrendered to the restless fire that had taunted him since he was a lad. He'd kept it hidden, especially from Granny.

Sara, with her flame-red hair and her willing body, coaxed the fire out of hiding. It licked through his veins, demanding the thing he shouldn't want.... freedom to do as he pleased.

If the problems magically disappeared. Oh, he could make them disappear. His mother had. She'd broken three hearts — Granny's, Grandpa's and his. Lucky's, too, come to think of it.

He wouldn't follow her lead. But pushing that little white vehicle to its limits gave him a dangerous taste of reckless abandon. And he liked it.

Once he turned onto the unpaved ranch road, he drove that stretch the way Lucky had, minding the ruts and watching for animals. Did Lucky have the fire in him, too? Maybe he'd ask. Or maybe he'd let it be.

"You looked like you were having fun."

"I was, yeah, but not as much as I will in a few minutes." His blood was hot, his jeans uncomfortable. "Would you be wearing underwear today?"

She laughed. "*Yes.* I always do. Last night was—"

"A surprise for me."

"Exactly. But since you've mentioned it, I'll take off my bra while we're driving, if that would make you happy."

"It'll make me go in a ditch."

"Then never mind." She took off his hat and laid it on the dash. Then she shook out her hair and ran her fingers through it.

Now that they'd blown out the chemical stink, he could smell the scent of her hair, a lemony one he remembered from the night before. It was stronger today. "Did you just wash your hair?"

"This morning, and now it has a mind of its own. "

"Smells good." He itched to get his fingers in those silky strands.

"Thanks. Hey, when we get there, don't do the cowboy thing and come around to let me out. It'll be faster if I get myself out."

"Okay. Fast is good."

Her chuckle was low and sexy. "Impatient, are we?"

"Driving like an eejit stirred me up."

"Stirred me up, too, and I wasn't the one at the wheel."

He sucked in a breath. "Good thing we're almost there." His pulse rate jumped as the turnoff came into view. What if Rance had come home for some reason? He said a prayer of thanks when the parking area turned out to be empty.

Sara unlatched her belt before he'd shut off the engine, and the minute he did she was out the door. "Meet you in there!"

In his haste to unfasten his belt he managed to jam it so the bleedin' thing wouldn't open. He was ready to wrench it from its moorings when it finally snapped free. Grabbing his hat, he lunged out of the car and banged his knee on the door. He slammed it shut so hard the wee vehicle shuddered.

Sending it a silent apology, he jogged to the steps and took them two at a time. She'd left the door open.

Her top lay on the closest end of the pool table and her bra dangled over the far end. A thump from the bedroom was followed by another — her boots hitting the hardwood. His vivid memory from last night sent an urgent message to his groin.

Closing the door, he left his hat on the rack next to it and began unbuttoning his shirt as he lengthened his stride. Sunlight streamed through windows left open on a clear day. The scent of pine mingled with the faint tang of woodsmoke from the hearth. Birds fluttered and chirped in the trees outside.

This. The visceral need for Sara pounded through his body, a primitive drumbeat that wouldn't be denied. But he wanted more.

He craved all of it — the cabin in the woods, the majestic mountains defining the horizon, his brother and the big loving family scattered over this vibrant landscape, the freedom to make love in the middle of the day to the woman of his dreams.

When he walked into the bedroom, she'd just stepped out of her jeans. Still holding them, she turned to him with a smile. "There you are. I thought I'd lost you."

"I wouldn't let that happen." It was the most he dared say. She didn't believe in miracles. Yet.

Stripping off his shirt, he dropped it and closed the distance between them, reaching for her, his body aching for contact.

The jeans fell from her fingers and rustled to the floor as she stepped into his arms, face lifted, eyes filled with an emotion she hadn't yet spoken. "Daylight is so special. Who knew?"

"I didn't." He combed his fingers through her fragrant hair, savored the sensation of her breasts yielding as he pressed her closer. "I was just excited that we'd have more time alone."

"It's a golden paradise." She shifted her hips, making room for her to unhook his belt from the buckle. "Except one of us is overdressed. Will you let me fix that for you?"

Her offer stole his breath. He wanted her hands on him, wanted that very much. His cock reacted to the prospect immediately. Releasing her, he stepped back. "I'm all yours."

"I need you to sit down so I can take off your boots."

"Yes, ma'am." Walking over to the bed, he turned and lowered himself to the mattress, wincing at the inevitable compression.

"Just for a minute. I can see you're uncomfortable." She crouched in front of him and began loosening the laces of his boot.

"I'm fine." The pleasure of watching her plump breasts quiver as she worked was balanced by the pain when his cock twitched in response.

"You're not. You made a face." She quickly unlaced his work boot and pulled it off, along with his sock. "Since I don't have your equipment, I don't know what that squeezed feeling is like, but I can use my imagination."

"It recovers quickly."

She glanced up, a sparkle in her green eyes. "That's a blessing." She unlaced the other boot and tugged it free. Then she straightened. "Go ahead and stand up."

When he did, he noticed a condom lying on the bedside table. "Only one?"

"I didn't want to presume. I slept in this morning but you couldn't because of your phone call." She came closer and reached for the button on his jeans.

"You think I'll take a nap?" Electricity shot through him as she slipped the button free and slowly pulled down the zipper. She had to work around his highly aroused *equipment*, as she'd called it.

"I'd be okay with that." She slid both hands behind his back.

"You would?"

"If that's what you need, of course I would." Tucking her hands inside the waistband of his briefs, she gripped his arse.

He almost came. "There'll be no napping going on." It came out as an angry growl as he fought for control. "I think y'know what I need, lass."

"I think I do." She pushed down both jeans and briefs. In the same motion she knelt before him.

Before he had the wits to stop her, she'd taken his cock in her mouth. He groaned. "I didn't mean...."

They were the last words he spoke before she robbed him of his vocabulary, his breath and his brain cells. The noble idea that he'd hold back and take control of the situation was short-lived.

In no time he began to shake like a sapling in the wind. Gasping and praying that he didn't black out, he gave up with a roar.

She stayed with him, taking all that he had to give, binding them together, whether she meant to or not. When he could finally breathe again, when the world stopped spinning, the truth shone through.

She'd claimed they had no chance at happiness, but every move she made told him she desperately wanted to be wrong.

28

Curled up next to Kieran, Sara laid her cheek against his warm chest and absorbed the steady beat of his generous heart. He'd insisted on returning the favor she'd bestowed on him, and she'd gladly let him have his way with her. His talented touch and clever tongue had left her gasping and sated... at least for now.

"That was lovely." She snuggled closer.

"'Tis a gift, sharing yourself with me, lass." He kissed the top of her head and stroked his fingers slowly through her hair. "I get far more than I give."

His manner of speaking charmed her as much as his virile body. "If we keep this up, we won't need any condoms."

"Oh, we need 'em. Much as I fancy the alternative, there's nothing like pushing deep and watching your eyes glow and your cheeks turn pink. It'll be even better in daylight."

"And we'll feel the soft breeze on our skin."

He chuckled. "Can't promise I'll notice a breeze on my arse when I'm in the moment."

"Have you ever done it outside?"

"I have not. Was thinking about it until Rance came up with this scheme."

"Lani was afraid we'd try that and be eaten by a bear. But my theory is you take a horseback ride out to your spot. If any critters show up, the horses will let you know in advance."

"Sounds like I need to learn how to ride a horse."

"You should."

"Taking a ride out into nature to make love would be a grand adventure."

"That's what I like about it."

"I'm ready for adventure."

It could have been a casual statement except for the resolute way he said it, as if he'd come to a decision. "Got a particular one in mind?"

"I do, yeah. More plane trips to Montana. I let the cost of a ticket hold me back. I don't have much in savings anymore, but I have skills. If Desiree bought my ticket, I could work off the debt during my stay. A place this massive can always use a fella who knows how to swing a hammer."

Her breath caught. Resourceful. And in line with Angie's thinking, although she wanted him fulltime. "How often would you come?"

"Depends on what I can negotiate with my employer. I'd love to make it over here two or three times a year. Maybe even more."

"What about Granny?"

"She should be fine if I'm only gone a couple of weeks at a stretch. It's not like she needs me to shop for her or take her places. Sure, she'd miss me, but Lucky and I have years to catch up on. She'd be all for that."

"Would you make a stop in New Jersey?"

"You know I would. But I could also time my visits for when you'll be here."

He'd just taken a flying leap forward. Her chest tightened. Was it anxiety or excitement? She couldn't tell. "Are you suggesting a long-distance relationship?"

"That I am." Cupping her chin, he coaxed her to look up at him. "What d'ya think?"

She gulped. "I thought you wanted the whole works — marriage, a family."

"It's still on the table."

"I—"

"But first we'd have to see how this setup turns out."

The jury was in. Her chest hurt because his plan wouldn't work for them the way he hoped. "I don't see it going well."

"How can you say that?" He frowned. "We haven't even—"

"It's brilliant for connecting with Lucky and the McLintocks. I'm sure they'll be excited about it. But we won't be seeing as much of each other as you imagine."

"Why not?"

"For starters, my next visit will be over the Christmas break."

"Ah. I see what you mean, there. I can't leave Granny at Christmas."

"I might make it back over the Easter weekend, too. I'll bet you can't leave then, either."

"No, but—"

"I used up a lot of vacation days on this trip. I might not get to the ranch again until the following Christmas."

"But this year you've already been here twice and you're coming again."

"I've been banking unused days ever since I started there. Once Dallas moved to Montana I had a hunch we'd be coming out sooner or later. I blew my saved days on the wedding and this trip."

"I didn't know that."

"There was no reason to explain it. I'll be concentrating on getting off for important holidays like Christmas now that my folks will be living out here."

"They're leaving Trenton?"

"Yep. They're selling the house. And probably their insurance agency, something I didn't realize until this minute. Wow, my folks are retiring. I didn't fully grasp that. Anyway, their announcement came after you left last night, and I didn't think to mention it."

"Well, then." He looked pleased about the news.

"Are you hoping I'll pull up stakes and follow them?"

"It might have crossed my mind."

"I won't, Kieran. I'm doing great with that company. To quit and move just because my folks are here and there's a chance you'll show up once in a while—"

"You're right, you're right."

"Your plan for making it to the ranch more often is inspired. Desiree will love it. Everyone will. But don't count on me being here when you make the trip. My job doesn't give me that kind of time or flexibility."

"I'm not sure mine will, either."

"What if it won't?"

"I'll find a job that will."

She knew that look. He'd had the same determined light in his eyes when he'd come into Hannigan's with a postcard in his shirt pocket. "And I'm sure you'll succeed."

"Forgive me for making assumptions, lass." He dragged in a breath. "I didn't understand you don't normally have this much time off and God knows I don't expect you to build your life around me."

"But we'll see each other." She traced the line of his mouth with her finger. "You'll fly into Newark and spend the night with me. I'll help you get over your jetlag and send you on your way." If that prospect made her heart ache, oh, well.

"That sounds better than an airport hotel."

"You can have another stopover on your way back. You can fill me in on the doings at the ranch."

"Be glad to." He smiled, but there was no sparkle in his eyes.

"Then when I make it to Dublin, you can show me around." Would he introduce her to Granny? Maybe not. The woman who'd raised him would sense instantly they were more than just friends.

"I have to believe we'll be able to coordinate a visit to the ranch... sometime."

"We will. Sometime. I'm sure this isn't the way you envisioned it when you had your brainstorm, but—"

"I'll take it." He gathered her close. "All I know is I can't let you go. I don't think you want to let me go, either."

"Of course I don't. We've found something special."

"And speaking of that…" He gently rolled her to her back. "We've spent way too much time talking about the future and not enough enjoying the present." He reached for the condom on the nightstand.

"Are you ready to have sex while a soft breeze caresses your butt?"

"A soft breeze can't compete with the pure joy of your hands gripping my arse and urging me on." Sitting back on his heels, he ripped open the package and rolled on the condom.

"How you talk."

"If I haven't told you how much I love that, I'm telling you now. I don't give a feck about the breeze. But hold onta me like you mean it and you'll make me a very happy fella."

"Count on it, cowboy."

29

Kieran's frustration was more than sexual, but at least he could relieve that much of it. Burying his cock deep and making Sara come, and come again, would do wonders, and he set about it with gusto.

As requested, she clamped her strong fingers on his arse and rose to meet each stroke. Any time now he'd feel the first ripple and he'd take her over the top, her cries music to his ears.

But no, she wasn't responding the way she had the other times. Feck it all, she was *thinking*. His fault. He'd had to tell her his brilliant plan, hadn't he? He'd started thoughts swirling in her head.

Thrusting once more, he paused, his gaze locked with hers. "You're not here. You're somewhere else."

She blinked, clearly not expecting that, but then the truth was in her eyes. "It's my problem, not yours."

He shook his head. "Our problem. Tell me."

"When you're at the ranch, and I can't be there..."

"That'll drive you crazy."

"I'll handle it."

"You won't have to." He lost another piece of his heart. "I won't be stopping in Newark, is all."

"You won't tell me you're—"

"Right. It's better if I—"

"No! I want you to tell me. I'll handle it."

Grand. Now they were arguing in the middle of the action. "Then I'll tell you." He returned to the gentle rhythm that had worked so well when they'd first made love. "I'll do better than that. I'll schedule the flight so I can spend the weekend with you. I'll do the same on the way back. We'll have four whole days together."

"That cuts into your time with Lucky."

"It was never just about Lucky." He rocked his hips slowly, coaxing her back to the moment, to this miracle they'd created together. "You were there first. It's always been you."

"And the ranch."

"And you." He kept moving and gradually the barriers slipped away.

"And this family."

"And you." There it was, the glow in her eyes, the faint tinge of pink on her cheeks.

"And the..." Her breath caught as the first twinge squeezed his cock. "The mountains."

He smiled. "And you." Shifting the angle, he thrust faster. He'd meant to wait, to give her two climaxes to his one. But instead he'd come with her. She liked it when he did that. So did he.

Holding her gaze, he gloried in her response, her body arching into his, her thighs trembling. Driving home, he let go, his rhythm matching hers. His gasps blended with her cries, and... a tune? The chime of his mobile?

Who would be calling him? And why?

"Is that... is that your—"

"Yeah." He gulped for air. "I'd better...." Holding the condom in place, he made a quick trip to the bathroom. While he was in there, the tune, a snatch of *Comin' Through the Rye*, stopped. A moment later the phone pinged with a message.

When he returned, Sara stood with his jeans in one hand and his mobile in the other. "They left a message."

"I heard."

"You do have good ears."

"My eyesight's perfect, too, if you're taking stock."

"I am, and I've decided your heart's way too big." She handed over his mobile.

"It matches my schlong." That earned him an eyeroll. He grinned and checked his mobile. "It's from Rance." He tapped the message.

Hi, buddy — got some bad news. Thunder's temporarily out of commission. Acted up on the way into town so I stopped by the dealership. Some tricky computer malfunction. They need to do a complete diagnostic, which means an overnight stay. Sorry. Thunder should be back in operation by tomorrow night, though. Hope you and Sara took advantage of me being at work.

He glanced at her. "Good thing we did."

"Thanks to you. And by the way, I looked at the time when I pulled your phone out. We should probably head over to the house."

"Hate to, since we won't have tonight."

"But we'll be together at the house and when you come back here, you can finally get some sleep. I'm sure you need it."

He laid the mobile on the bedside table and gathered her close. "I need you."

"And I need you." She gazed up at him. "I've tried to pretend that comes as a big surprise, but a part of me always knew I'd fall like a ton of bricks."

"Have you ever seen a ton of bricks fall?"

She smiled and shook her head. "Have you?"

"I did, yeah. A ton is about four hundred and fifty bricks, or about a hundred square meters. I took part in a demolition once. A ton of bricks coming down makes your ears ring."

She wound her arms around his neck. "When you make love to me, my ears ring. Must be all those bricks falling."

"Must be." He gave in to the urge to kiss her, just once more, and then he didn't want to let her go.

But he had to. He might as well get used to it. His future would be filled with moments of pulling her close and letting her go. It wasn't what he wanted, but it was better than nothing.

30

Sara had steered clear of drama classes in high school, leaving that activity to Lani. As she spent a tortuous evening with her family while trying not to act like she was sleeping with Kieran, she was convinced everyone knew and had decided not to bring it up.

More than once she was tempted to confess, just to relieve the pressure. But then what? Rance's scheme would collapse. If they all saw right through her and had decided to look the other way, she could continue to enjoy a few hours with Kieran every night until the week was over.

She had a moment of panic when he started toward the front door at the end of the evening. He'd have to drive that little white car back to Rance's cabin by himself. What if he ran into a problem? Or forgot and drove on the left when someone was coming from the other direction?

No one else seemed concerned, especially him. He promised to be back early in the morning so he and Desiree could prep for another call to his grandmother. On the way out he tipped his hat. Adorable.

After he left, everyone said good night. Desiree and Andy headed toward their bedroom and her parents split off toward the kids' wing.

Sara braced herself as she and Lani trailed behind. If her parents planned to say anything, this would be the moment.

They didn't. Bidding her and Lani goodnight, they went into their bedroom and closed the door.

She followed Lani in and pushed the door shut with a sigh of relief. "That was awful. I'm sure they all know."

"They might, but they might not." Lani sat on the edge of her bed. "I can't tell for sure. *I* think you're acting weird, but then I'm in on it. I'm probably seeing things they don't notice."

"Well, everyone can get an uninterrupted night's sleep for a change, because Thunder's in the shop so Rance and I won't be doing the switch."

"In the shop?" Lani sounded disappointed. Odd. "For how long?"

"Just until tomorrow."

"That's good."

"Good? Why do you care?"

"Because… I hate to admit it, but you two seem to be right for each other. Which is sad because it can't work out, but at least you'll have this week to remember."

"We'll have more than this week."

"What?" She sat up straighter.

"He has a new plan, although he didn't bring it up tonight. He probably wants to speak to Desiree alone, first."

"What plan?"

She outlined his strategy and included the part about weekend layovers in New Jersey.

Lani looked less than enthusiastic. "I can see why he wants to spend more time here, but trying to keep things going with you... that's messed up."

"I'd rather have him a few days a year than not at all."

"Would you really? And what about the rest of the year? Will you date?"

"I'll have to see how it goes." The answer was no and hell no, but she wouldn't say that to Lani. She couldn't imagine wanting anyone else.

"Would you be okay with him dating?"

Her stomach churned. "If that's what he wants."

"I didn't ask that. Would you be able to stand it?"

"He wouldn't date. That's not like him."

"Oh, Sara. The whole thing's a terrible idea. You'll both be miserable for ninety-eight percent of the time. That's not a life. You need to set each other free."

"But how can I? He'll follow through on his plan. I saw the look in his eye when he came up with the sweat equity idea. Angie will snap up that offer in a heartbeat. And he should do it. Spending short periods of time is a great compromise."

"Except knowing he's here will be hell on you. Not only that, but when you do visit, you'll have to listen to the family talk about him. Even our folks will. If they build a cabin with Angie's help, Kieran might very well work on it, too."

Sara groaned and fell back on the bed. "This is a fecking nightmare."

"Fecking?"

"It's what they say over there, like we would say effing. I like it."

"I kinda do, too. You've been fascinated by Ireland for a long time, even when we were kids. I always thought you took the job with Adventuring Travel mostly because it would get you to Ireland."

"That was a big part of it. And next year I'll get to go. I'll see Kieran on that trip, too."

"For all of one night?"

"Maybe more. Depends on what else I'm required to do."

"You could marry him and live there the rest of your life."

"No, I couldn't."

"Why not?"

"Because I'm smart enough to know that I've romanticized the place."

"Hard not to. You're in the business of promoting it."

"Yep. But living in a tiny village and trying to carve out a satisfying career like what I have now would be tough if not impossible. I won't give up everything for a man. I'm grateful to our parents for teaching us that."

"You know what? This is all Dallas's fault."

That made her laugh. "No, it's not."

"Yes, it is! He's the one who *had* to move to a tiny rural fire department and was *so* excited to live in cowboy country. If he'd stayed in Trenton like a normal person, none of this would have happened."

"I guess he did start it. And look at how happy he is. Trent, too. They're both eating up this ranch life. So are Mom and Dad. I haven't seen them laugh and joke this much in years."

"Which makes us odd women out."

Sara turned her head to gaze at her sister. "I won't fold if you won't."

"I'm not leaving Trenton."

Sara reached a hand across the space between the two beds. "Pinkie swear?"

"Pinkie swear." She hooked her little finger with Sara's. "That said, you're still fecked, sis."

_31_

Maybe Sara was right that he'd needed sleep. Kieran had intended to stay up until Rance came home from the Buffalo, but he'd only had enough energy to send Granny several texts with pictures attached.

He'd told her that Lucky had the one of their mother's grave and would send it to her soon. After that he couldn't keep his eyes open, so he'd gone to bed.

Next thing he knew it was morning, but this time he woke up on his own, even before Rance. For a moment he lay there listening to the birds and gazing out the window at the tall pines not far from the cabin. He'd always had trouble imagining fairies back home, but he could feel them here.

Dressing in his jeans and a T-shirt, he went out to the kitchen and took the liberty of making coffee. Either the noise or the smell woke Rance. A floorboard creaked in the other bedroom, the one with a couch in it.

Every time Kieran glanced at that couch he felt guilty, but Rance insisted it was comfortable. Since the arrangement was the only way Kieran had a decent place to bring Sara, he'd make sure his host knew how much the sacrifice meant to him.

Rance appeared wearing sweatpants and nothing else. He scratched his chest and yawned. "Sorry about Thunder crappin' out on us, buddy."

"It might have been a blessing. Sara told me I needed sleep and I guess she was right."

"I think so. You were conked out when I came home."

"And woke up on my own this time. Fancy a cup?"

"Sure."

He poured two mugs and handed one to Rance. "Do you have a workout room somewhere?"

"I do." Rance took a sip. "I enclosed my back porch a while back and that's where I have my bench. Want to use it?"

"Don't know that I have time, but thanks for the offer. I figured you did. You don't build muscle like that bartending."

"That's for sure. Derek — that's Bret and Gil's dad — has been on all of us to stay in shape ever since I can remember. When we were kids he'd bring us weights and jump ropes and stuff whenever he visited." He took another swallow.

"For everyone?"

"That's the kind of guy he is. We're all glad he decided to move back to Wagon Train."

"I can't believe Andy's happy, though."

"Nah, he's cool. He's figured out the dads aren't competition. Nick's a better dancer than Andy, Steven's loaded, and Derek can bench-press two-twenty, but Mom doesn't care about any of that. Andy's the only one for her."

"Savage."

"You said it." Rance grinned. "This family's definitely savage. So how did things go at the cemetery? Did you get your picture?"

"Thanks for reminding me. Lucky said he'd send the revised version to me and Granny when he got it. I left my mobile in the bedroom." Hurrying out of the kitchen, he picked it up from the bedside table. He had a text from Sara, one from Lucky and six from Granny.

He followed his heart and opened Sara's first. *You did great last night. I was a hot mess. Do you want to try a practice ride today? Just around the yard, not on a trail. If you want to, I'll text Marsh and ask if we can borrow Pie. He's a very sweet horse. You'll like him.*

Smiling, he read the text at least three times, maybe more. He could hear her voice, see the eagerness in her expression, feel the love. She didn't have to say it. He could tell by the way—

"Everything okay?"

He looked up. Rance stood in the doorway looking anxious. "Sorry! Got distracted. Sara's asking if I want to ride Pie around the yard today."

"You should definitely do that." Rance's frown disappeared. "*Pie* is short for *Sweetie-Pie*, Jimmy Stewart's favorite horse. That horse is long gone but this one looks just like him."

"Are you slagging me, mate?"

"Swear to God. Years ago Mom decided to find lookalikes for famous horses."

"It's not just Lucky's Silver, then?"

"Heck, no. We all have famous ones. Mine's Diablo, a black and white paint just like the Cisco

Kid rode. Mom's got Trigger. Angie has Buttermilk. Savage, right?"

"Pure savage. I haven't made it to the barn, yet, but now I can't wait."

"They'll be out in the pasture by the time you get down there, but Sara can point them out to you. She knows 'em all."

"But she was only here for a week back in February. How did she have time to—"

"She made good use of that week, taking pictures of each horse so she wouldn't forget. She's been taking riding lessons back home. Found someone who taught Western. She's a lot more fascinated and attached to the ranch, and us, than she'll admit."

"It's not surprising. Being here, I feel like...." He paused. "When I was about seven, a carnival came to town. I loved it all — the rides, the candy floss, the lights, the music. Rowdy Ranch feels like that."

Rance nodded. "I used to take this place for granted. But when Mav was born — Jess and Beau's kid — I had an inkling I was part of something cool. The realization hit me full force when Andy moved in. He appreciated it so much that I saw it through his eyes. Now I don't let a day go by without giving thanks for... everything."

"I envy you."

Rance's gaze intensified. "You belong here, buddy. I feel it in my bones. Is there any way—"

"I won't leave Granny. But I've come up with a plan." He quickly outlined his idea.

"That's brilliant. Mom will go for it in a heartbeat. Now if only Sara would relocate, the two of you could—"

"I can't ask it of her. She's five years into her career with that travel company. I'd only be around for a couple of weeks here and there. It's not a good deal."

"I guess not."

He glanced at the time on his mobile. "I need to get moving. I promised Desiree I'd be there early to get ready for the call."

"While you shower, I'll throw something together for breakfast."

"Thanks. Do you need a ride to work? After the call I can—"

"Clint's picking me up. Don't worry about me. Text Sara and then jump in the shower."

He sent Sara a thumbs up, then shaved and showered quick as he could. Over a simple breakfast of cereal and toast, he and Rance studied the digitally altered picture of Freya Noreen Haggerty's grave.

"Molly did a damned good job," Rance said. "Tell me the story the way you'll tell it to Granny, in case I ever talk to her."

"I'm sure you will. And I've told her the truth, that when the father didn't show up, Desiree stepped in. I'm leaving out that she didn't give her real name. I think knowing that would bring Granny unnecessary pain, like she was living like a criminal."

"I agree. Well done."

"I sent her some other pictures last night before I went to bed. You need to see how she texts." He explained her method and turned his mobile over to Rance.

By the time he got to the sixth one, tears of laughter were streaming down his face and catching on his beard stubble. "There's *gotta* be a way to get her over here."

Kieran sighed. "You heard what Lucky said. If I told her this is where I want to spend the rest of my life, but I'll stay in Ireland for her, she'd start packing. But I'd never do such a thing."

"Of course not. But what if she'd love it here?"

"What if the stress of getting on a plane for the first time in her life gave her a heart attack?"

"You'd never been on a plane, either. Were you stressed about it?"

"I thought it was pure craic, but I'm fifty years younger. And I have my mother's fire. Granny doesn't have it."

"I dunno. She sent you a volcano, fireworks and a shooting star. That looks damned fiery to me. And the crossed swords isn't exactly a symbol of tranquility."

"Like I said, her finger slips."

"So you say. It could also be the real Granny making a stealth appearance."

"Wishful thinking, mate." He polished off his coffee and grabbed his mobile. "Let me know about Thunder."

"I will, and just so you know, I'll do the double drive tonight. I'm not taking a chance on Sara getting stuck."

"Appreciate it." He hadn't remembered that she'd decided to make the trip on her own, but with Thunder having computer issues, he was glad Rance would be in charge.

Desiree, dressed in jeans and a plaid shirt, was waiting for him in Rowdy Roost. Hopping down from a bar stool, she gave him a hug. "Lucky's running a little late."

"Let me text Granny and tell her." He got out his mobile and typed a short message. "Done." He laid it on the bar to keep it handy for the call. "This gives me a chance to ask you about something."

She smiled. "Go for it." As he launched into his plan, her smile grew. When he finished she gave him another hug. "I love it. Angie will, too. She's talked about how much she'd like to have you as part of her crew."

"She has?"

"She's expanding the business and you'd be a valuable addition. She'll be glad to have you whenever you can manage it."

"That's grand news. I'll mention it to her first chance I get, then."

"Do that." She studied him, her expression calm. "I have something to say, too. I know what Rance has been up to."

His breath whooshed out and his face heated. He wasn't surprised that she'd found out, just scundered. "He's only trying to help. If you're upset, blame me. I could've told him no, but—"

"I'm not upset. You and Sara are consenting adults caught in an awkward set of circumstances. It's your business how you handle the situation. Which is what I told her this morning."

"You've talked to her?"

"We just happened to have a moment alone so I grabbed my chance. She told me to blame her."

"Ah, no, never her. She—"

"I'm not blaming anyone. Like I said, it's your business."

Meeting her gaze, he dragged in a breath. "Thank you." And that was how a legend conducted herself when faced with such things. He'd admired her before. Now his regard bordered on worship.

She smiled. "You're welcome."

"When did you find out?"

"I've known from the beginning. I didn't believe for a minute that Rance felt 'left out'." She made air quotes. "He and Lucky had their relationship tested back in February and they came out of it stronger than ever."

"That's what he told Lucky and Oksana when they gave us a lift to his cabin."

She nodded. "I figured he would. And Sara told me Lani's in on it."

"She is. Had to be."

"Rance must be in his element playing matchmaker and ringmaster at the same time."

"He's likely to fail at the matchmaking part. What about Sara's folks? Do they know?"

"I'm not sure. Andy does because we don't keep secrets from each other. But I see no reason to mention it to Vanessa and Harry unless they bring it up."

"I just hope they realize ..." He fumbled for the right words. "Sara means the world to me. I would never—"

"We can all see that. And she feels the same about you. It's unfortunate that... well, you're in a no-win situation, aren't you?"

"I can't speak for Sara, but I've been blessed. Spending this time with her makes me the most fortunate fella alive."

Desiree's eyes lit up. "Nicely put. Which brings me to something else. When I mentioned something about this upcoming call, she laughed and said she wished she could be a mouse in the corner. And I thought why not?"

"I can't think of any reason. I didn't know she wanted to listen in."

"She's a part of the story, a player from the get-go. Naturally she's curious to hear how it goes between me and your granny."

"Then she should be here."

"Great. I said I'd text her if you gave the okay." She pulled out her mobile.

He should have thought of it himself. He wished he could introduce her to his oul dear and say exactly how he felt about her. Sara and Granny were the two most important women in his life and they should know each other. Would that ever happen?

32

Sara took her phone out to the front porch where Lani sat reading a manuscript. Their parents were at the building site with Angie so they could discuss cabin design and placement.

Sara wasn't about to go with them when she had the possibility of listening to the phone call. Lani didn't go because she was in mourning for the family home in Trenton and was pretending the cabin project was a mirage.

When the text came from Desiree, Sara leaped up. "He said yes! I get to listen in."

"Wish I could. This manuscript is deadly dull."

"I could ask Kieran if you—"

"No, don't. It's not a performance. That's Lucky's truck coming around the bend, so you'd better get in there."

"I'll wait for him. I want to explain why I'm going in."

"Yeah, otherwise he might think you're doing the big reveal."

"That would be a mistake."

"I think so, too. You — oh, dear God. Rance is with him."

"What's so bad about that?"

"He asked if I wanted to go riding this morning before he had to go in to work and I told him I was too busy."

"You are busy. You're reading a manuscript."

"And wasting my time. We won't be buying it."

"Then go riding."

"But if I do, he'll think... oh, what the hell does it matter what he thinks? I'm going." She handed the manuscript to Sara. "Would you please take this in for me?"

"You bet." She pressed her lips together to keep from smirking. Would Lani ever admit she had a crush on Rance? Then again, nothing could come of it, so maybe her sister was smart to resist.

While Lani hurried to catch up with Rance as he headed for the barn, Lucky turned toward the porch steps, his long legs making quick work of the distance. "Hey, Sara."

"Hey, Lucky. I'm going in as a silent observer today."

"Oh?" He climbed the steps.

"Kieran said I could and I'm dying to see the meeting of Desiree and Granny.

"He won't mention you're there?"

"Nope. I'm just eavesdropping."

"I won't be saying much, either. This is Mom's turn." Crossing the porch, he held the door for her.

"When does Oksana get her turn?"

"Tomorrow. We've got somebody covering the shop so we can both be on the call. We don't want to overload Granny's circuits and she and Mom will have a lot to say to each other." He gestured toward the kitchen. "Let's take the shortcut."

She made a quick right and he followed. "By the way, why didn't Rance ride over with Kieran since they're in the same cabin?"

"He wasn't ready when Kieran had to leave, so he called me. I just happened to be running late or he would've been SOL."

"Why didn't you park by the back door of Rowdy Roost like before?"

"I was gonna. Then Rance saw Lani sitting on the porch and asked me to park where she could see him get out."

Sara gave a hoot of laughter. "It worked. She decided to go riding, after all."

"Saw that." He chuckled.

"I'm worried she'll break his heart."

"He's a big boy. He knows she's set on living back East. He'll either change her mind or learn the hard way that she's not the one. What's that you're taking in with you? Did someone write up a script for this call?"

"It's a boring manuscript. Lani's catching up on submissions. By the way, she was really bummed her company didn't get Oksana's book."

"They had no chance once it turned into a bidding war."

"Yeah, they have a limited budget. But she loves working there." She pushed open the swinging bar doors and Kieran turned away from the bar and started toward them.

His sheepish grin said it all. Desiree had told him she knew everything. He glanced at her. "Hey."

"Hey, yourself."

Then he turned to Lucky. "Well, bro, we didn't fool your mom, after all. She knew Rance was making up that story."

"I might've a few years ago," Desiree called from her seat at the bar. "But not after you two had it out back in February."

"So here's the question." Lucky's gaze moved from Kieran to Sara. "Do we tell Rance that's she's known all along? Because he's so proud of this scheme that I kinda hate to burst his bubble."

"If you don't want to tell him, I'll keep my mouth shut," Desiree said from her perch on a bar stool, "but let's table that until later, okay? Time's a-wasting."

"Yes, ma'am. Sorry I'm a little late." Lucky hurried over toward the bar, which looked to be operation central. He took a stool one away from Desiree, clearly leaving the middle one for Kieran, who hadn't followed him over.

Sara made a shooing motion. "Go on ahead. I'll find a place to sit."

"I'm glad you're here. I should have thought of it."

"Never mind. Just—"

"Come sit by me, Sara." Desiree turned and patted the bar stool beside her. "It's not like we're on video. You'll be fine."

"Okay, thanks." She gave Kieran a quick smile and made for her designated spot.

"Want anything?" he called after her. "Water, soda—"

"I'm good, thanks."

"He's besotted," Desiree murmured.

"Mm-hm." So was she.

Pulling a red bandana from her back pocket, Desiree laid it on the bar. "Just in case I get weepy."

"Oh." Sara checked her pockets. No tissues.

"Use a napkin from the holder if you need it." Desiree gestured toward a black metal dispenser not far away.

"Got it."

"I'm dialing." Kieran picked up his phone and tapped the screen.

After only one ring, a woman's voice boomed out. "Kieran, my boy! Saints alive, so many pictures you sent me!"

"Too many, Granny?"

Sara melted at the gentle teasing note in his voice.

"*Never*. Keep 'em comin', laddie! Such a beautiful place. And ya made it to the cemetery, you and Lucky. And ya took flowers, didn't ya now?"

"We did."

"It's a grand stone my Freya has." Her voice trembled a little. "And one of you on either side of it, lookin' so fine. Anyone can see you're brothers."

"I'm glad you liked it."

"Loved it, I did. Showed it all around. Must've been three of you there, since I saw three bouquets. Was the third one takin' the picture?"

Sara's breath hitched as she made googly eyes at Kieran and Lucky. Busted!

"I was." Desiree. said.

Whew. Problem solved.

"Is that Desiree talkin'?"

"Yes, it is, Mrs. Haggerty. I don't feel right calling you granny."

"Didn't that boy tell you my Christian name?"

"I might have missed it."

"'Tis Bridget. You can call me that. Everyone does, apart from him. Oh, Desiree, luv, I can't tell you how much it means, what you did."

"I was supposed to be there."

"Of course you were. It was God's will that you were there with my Freya. Can you tell me... if you can remember...." Her voice faltered.

"Like it was yesterday. We shared a room."

"Truly? Side by side? She wasn't alone then?"

"No. We talked."

"About her home? About County Kildare? Was she missin'...." There was a soft gulp on the other end.

"I'm sure she was." Desiree wadded up the bandana in her hand, crushing it in her fist. "She had big plans."

"She always did, that one." Sorrow laced every syllable.

"They were good plans, Bridget. For her and the baby." Desiree's voice grew husky. "I've been where she was. Alone, with a baby. I would've helped her."

"I know ya would, luv." Her voice trembled. "Friends, you'da been. Grand friends. She was...."

"Amazing."

No words came through, just the sound of a tissue being ripped from the box and soft sobs.

Sara peeked over at Desiree. Her cheeks were wet but the bandana remained clenched in her fist. She stared straight ahead at an image only she could see.

Then she took a deep breath. "We have to remember the living, Bridget." She swiped at her face with the wad of red cloth. "We have Lucky."

Bridget blew her nose. "Praise God we have that boy." She sounded much stronger. "Lucky, are you there?"

"I'm here, Granny." His voice was a little ragged around the edges, too.

"You're a gift to Desiree and she's a gift to you. Don't you ever forget it."

"I won't, Granny."

"And you have another gift, another great blessing. Oksana, your wife. Is she there?"

"No. We decided—"

"Why isn't she there?"

"We didn't want to have too many people at once."

"Why?"

"Well, we thought—"

"Ah. Ya thought your oul granny couldn't take it."

Lucky exchanged a look with Kieran.

"There's another reason," Kieran said. "They have that bookshop in town and Oksana needed to be down there today to keep things in order."

"Nice try, boyo. Next time ya call, bring as many as will come. Send me a list of names and pictures so I can learn who's who. I taught school, ya know. I'm good with names and faces."

"You taught school?"

"Quit when your mum left for America. Knew in my bones she wasn't comin' back."

"You never told me."

"What's the use? Doesn't matter."

"I'd like to hear about it."

"Maybe sometime. Can I talk to Desiree some more? I have somethin' ta ask her."

Kieran turned the phone in her direction.

"I'm here, Bridget."

"Has Kieran met any nice girls since he's been there? Because he might not tell me if he has."

Desiree sat back on her stool. "Um, well…" She glanced at Kieran and then over her shoulder at Sara. "I—"

"I'm askin' because that boyo is thirty-two and it's time for him to settle down. None of the village girls are for him and he wouldn't be happy with a city girl. I was hopin' he'd meet someone over there."

Kieran turned the phone back in his direction. "Maybe we should talk about this another time."

"I'm talkin' about it now because I've been havin' crazy dreams that you found someone. I thought she might be the one who brought the other flowers, the one that took the picture. But Desiree says she did it."

"Well, she—"

"Did she take the others, too, then? The ones in the bookshop?"

"I'm not sure who—"

"There's one where you're looking in the camera and whoever's taking the picture is someone you care about."

"Granny, it's getting late, and we should probably—"

"You're hiding somethin', boyo. You can't fool your oul granny. You've found someone. And I want ta know all about her."

_33_

Sweat trickled down the back of Kieran's neck as he stared at his mobile and tried to find a way out of this without telling an outright lie. That wouldn't work, anyway. She knew him too well.

Desiree tapped him on the shoulder and motioned for him to turn the mobile in her direction. "Bridget, I think you and Kieran need to continue this conversation in private, so Lucky and I will say goodbye for now."

"Ya have the right of it, luv. I'll talk to ya again soon. I'll never forget the nice things ya said about my Freya. I wisht ya could've been friends."

"We were friends. Not for long, but friends all the same. Take care."

Lucky leaned toward the phone. "I'm off to the bookshop, Granny. I'll bring Oksana tomorrow."

"Ya do that, my boy. Give her my love when ya see her."

"I will." He squeezed Kieran's shoulder before following Desiree.

Sara slipped off her bar stool, mouthed _good luck_ and started after them.

Grabbing her hand, he shook his head.

Her eyes widened as he drew her closer. "Granny, your instincts are right, as always. I've met someone. Her name is Sara Armstrong, and she's standing right here beside me."

"I knew it! Sara, you say? 'Tis a grand name. Tell me about yerself, Sara, luv. How old are you?"

She cleared her throat. "I'm twenty-six, Mrs. Haggerty."

"Ah, no, call me granny. Or Bridget, but if you're twenty-six I'm old enough to be your granny."

"Then granny it is." Her voice was a little wobbly. "I live in New Jersey and I work for a travel company. I met Kieran because I'm in town visiting my brothers."

"Do ya fancy him, then?"

"I do, but there's a problem. I need to stay in New Jersey for my work and Kieran needs to stay in Ireland for... his work."

"Not just his work, luv. It's me keepin' him here. He's been a comfort, until I see the years slippin' by and he's thirty-two and no prospects. Not even a nibble."

He'd had enough of such talk. "Thirty-two isn't old. I have plenty of time to—"

"'Tis me, too, laddie. I want ya settled before I step out for tea. Wouldn't mind a great grandchild along the way."

"Lucky and Oksana might help you with that."

"So they might. Would be grand to be around if that happens. Is Wagon Train near to New Jersey?"

He'd recently looked it up in case driving was an option. It wasn't. "It's almost four thousand kilometers."

"So if ya lived in New Jersey with Sara, then—"

"I'll not be living in New Jersey, Granny." He caught Sara's attention and held her gaze. "I'll be living in County Kildare. I'll visit Rowdy Ranch. I'll stop by and see Sara, but—"

"That's no good, my boy. Do ya fancy Sara?"

"Yes, but—"

"Would she marry ya, then?"

He soaked up the compassion in Sara's eyes and gave the best answer he could come up with. "Under different circumstances, I believe she would."

Her smile told him he'd done a decent job.

"You're a smart fella, as smart or smarter than yer mum. Find a way to change the circumstances."

"I won't leave you, Granny."

"Looks like ya hafta take me with ya, then."

He gasped. "What?"

"Won't be a stroll through the rose garden, lad. Get carsick something awful unless all the windows are down. Can't put the windows down on a plane."

"Carsick? I didn't know that, either."

"'Tis why I live in a village where I can walk to everythin' when the weather's good. Wherever ya plant me over there, Wagon Train or New Jersey, I won't be leavin'. Be sure of that. Not goin' through that plane trip more than once."

"I'll not be *planting* you anywhere. This is crazy. You're where you need to be."

"You're not hearin' me, my boy. I'm pushin' ya out of the nest. And I'll be jumpin' out with ya. Sara, luv, don't know if I'll be meetin' ya in New Jersey or Wagon Train, but it'll be a grand day either way. I'll be hangin' up, now." She disconnected.

Kieran laid his mobile on the bar. Then he looked at Sara, his head spinning. "What just happened?"

"I think that's called throwing down the gauntlet."

"She's never talked like that before. She never said she was worried that I wouldn't get married. I didn't know her only problem was carsickness, for God's sake! I thought she was afraid to leave her comfort zone."

"Vomiting in the car isn't in anybody's comfort zone."

"Don't they have stuff you can take?"

"Now they do, but I doubt they had it when she was a kid. She probably had a traumatic experience when she was young and another one when she took a chance by going on her honeymoon."

"How can I ask her to suffer through a major trip, then?"

"You have no choice. She sees you stagnating where you are and she knows you won't go without her. You'll have to slay this dragon together. With the help of a strong anti-nausea drug."

"Why now?"

She reached over and took his hand in both of hers. "You know the answer. You showed her Rowdy Ranch. And Lucky. She wants that life for you, and maybe for herself."

"Or New Jersey and a granddaughter-in-law. She'd go with that option, too."

She shook her head. "It's not an option and you know it."

"Do I?" His gut tightened. "My skills would get me hired there. I haven't studied the immigration laws but I think marrying you would allow me to stay in the country."

Her gaze softened. "You don't belong in Trenton. And neither does she."

"I belong with you, damn it. If that means living in Trenton, I'll do that. Your folks are selling their house, right? Granny and I can buy it."

"How? Didn't you use all your savings for this trip?"

"That I did, but she'll be selling her house. I doubt it'll bring enough to buy your folks' place free and clear, but it'll do for a downpayment. What do you say? Will you marry me?"

She didn't answer, but she didn't have to. The sadness in her eyes told him all he needed to know.

He dragged in a breath. "I can guess why you won't, but please tell me, anyway."

"The thing is, I want to say yes."

"Then say it! We can be happy there. You'll have your great job, I'll surely find work in such a massive city, and we'll take holidays at Rowdy Ranch."

"And what about Granny? She'd never get to Rowdy Ranch."

"I suppose that's true. Unless I drive her the whole distance with the windows down."

"She'd have no one but us there and have to make new friends in a city environment, which she isn't used to. Everyone drives or takes public transportation. Riding with the windows down would be cold in winter, hot in summer and in heavy traffic she'd be breathing car exhaust."

"She'd have the open window problem at Rowdy Ranch, too."

"But not as much. No fumes to speak of, and I can picture Rance giving her a ride with the windows down and the heater on in winter, or the A/C in the summer. She'd have a built-in social group from the get-go and the town will feel something like her village back home. Plus her grandson's here."

"I can't argue with any of it. She'd be treated like a queen."

"And you'll be treated like a prince. Angie wanted to offer you a fulltime job if you'd consider moving. I asked her to hold off."

"Why?"

"I was afraid it would stress you out. You'd want to take it but couldn't because of your granny."

"That was kind of you."

"But you've ended up stressed out, anyway."

"How about this? I settle Granny in at Rowdy Ranch where she has folks around her and her other grandson. Then I come live with you in New Jersey."

She groaned. "Don't do this to me!"

"Do what?"

"Keep tempting me with scenarios that would almost work."

"What's wrong with this one? Granny's happy and we're both happy."

"Granny's used to seeing you all the time. She won't be happy if she only has you a week or two during the year."

"But she'd have Lucky and everyone else."

"She wouldn't have you. You're irreplaceable. And you wouldn't have her. Don't tell me that wouldn't be tough on you because I know better."

"What will be tough on me is not having you."

"Look, if you're living here, I'll figure out a way to visit more often. I'll find you cheap fares to come and see me. This ranch is where you both belong."

She was right that Granny would be happy here. He'd tried to tell himself she'd be fine in Trenton but she wouldn't.

Sara was also right about him. He'd always preferred small towns to big cities and he loved Rowdy Ranch. But how much of that was the ranch and how much was Sara? He dreaded finding out the answer.

<u>34</u>

Getting Kieran on a horse for the first time was exactly the kind of activity the situation called for. Sara's heart was slowly cracking down the middle, but introducing him to an activity he'd cherish for the rest of his life was good juju and they could both use some of that.

Even better, Lani and Rance were riding in as she and Kieran walked toward the barn. She'd call it serendipity, but Kieran might not be ready to share the news with them.

She gave them a wave as they headed to the hitching post in front of the barn. "Do you want to say something or keep it to ourselves?"

"Might as well tell 'em, since I texted it to Lucky and Desiree."

"But did you give them permission to tell others?"

"Didn't think to. Just said we were going to the barn and I'd fill them in on the details next time we saw each other."

"Then Andy and Oksana will get the story, but it'll stop there until you give the okay. I've been around this crowd long enough to know that."

"Lani and Rance have stuck by us. They deserve to hear it before the others."

"I think so, too. Hey, guys!" she called out as they approached the hitching post.

They each looked up and responded with *hey* but they weren't talking to each other. Instead they concentrated on the task, flipping the stirrups up on the saddles and loosening the girths.

Lani had ridden Buttermilk, Angie's horse. Angie was happy to loan her out, but Lani wasn't happy right now and neither was Rance.

Sara waded into the tense atmosphere. "Did you guys have a problem out there?"

"*He's* the problem." Lani gestured toward Rance. "He thinks he knows everything."

"No, I don't, Lani-Lou. I simply—"

"Don't call me that."

"But it's cute. Middle names don't get enough respect and Louise is—"

"Not the favorite part of my name, okay?" She turned to Sara. "See what I mean? He slaps a nickname on me to prove how clever he is. *Not*."

Sara glanced back at Kieran. "Maybe this isn't the time."

"I think it is. Unless you need to get goin', Rance. When is Clint givin' you a lift?" His accent was more pronounced after talking to his granny, who had a much stronger accent. Endearing.

Rance turned, one hand on his saddle. "He's picking me up here in another hour or so. Has something happened, buddy?"

"It has, yeah. Granny wants to switch countries."

Rance and Lani both gasped, but Rance got in the first question. "*Countries*? Are you sure she didn't say *counties*?"

"She knows what she's sayin, mate. She's willin' to come to New Jersey or Wagon Train, but—"

"*New Jersey*?" Lani glanced at Sara. "Why would she come there?"

"Steady, sis. She's not coming to New Jersey. Kieran and I talked it out. He and Granny will be relocating, but to Rowdy Ranch."

"Hot damn. That's a wonderful surprise." Rance grinned and held out his hand to Kieran. "Welcome to the Ponderosa, buddy." Then his gaze flicked to Sara. "Although you two don't seem overjoyed."

Giving a little shrug, she looked at Kieran. "We talked about the New Jersey option, but Granny would be miserable and Kieran and I aren't willing to sacrifice her happiness so that we can be together. Not to mention Kieran really belongs here with the McLintocks."

"There's gotta be a tasty option for you out here, Sara." Rance's tone was more intense than usual. What had happened on the trail must have knocked him off kilter. "We just haven't thought of it."

Lani whirled toward him. "Don't you dare suggest that she give up a career she loves, something she's wanted for years and invested her heart and soul into, so she can—"

"But what if there's something better out here? An exciting opportunity that would give her even more chance to develop her talents? Maybe it's a long shot, but isn't it worth investigating? Why can't she and Kieran have it all?"

"Because this is *real life*, Rance." Lani's eyes blazed. "This isn't like one of your mom's books where the good people win, the bad people get punished and everybody's hunky-dory at the end. Grow up."

"Ouch." Rance gave her a half-hearted smile. Then he looked at Sara, clearly chastened. "Please know that I respect your choices."

"I know you do." She appreciated Lani's support, but Rance wasn't a chauvinistic jerk who thought all women should follow blindly when a man crooked his finger.

Evidently Lani had just figured that out. She took a shaky breath. "I'm sorry, Rance. That's a hot button for me."

"I'm aware. I shouldn't have pushed it." He offered his hand. "Friends?"

"Friends." She shook it quickly and looked away. "We need to finish tending to these patient horses."

"I know, right?" Rance's laugh sounded hollow. "Diablo's usually a pain in the ass. I think you intimidate him." He looked at Kieran. "You're here for Pie, I take it."

"That's the plan."

"He's in his stall. Buck kept him in this morning so he'd be handy. Buck would probably appreciate it if you guys would turn him out when you're done."

"We will." Sara walked over to Lani and gave her a hug. "We'll talk soon."

"Definitely."

Kieran didn't speak until they were inside the barn on their way to Pie's stall. "I think he needs to give up."

"On Lani?"

"Yeah. She thinks he's an eejit."

"That's what she tells herself because she's afraid he could make her give up everything."

"After what she said?"

"Especially after what she said." Sara lowered her voice. "That was fear talking."

"Are you afraid I'd do that?"

She stopped next to Pie's stall. "No. You were ready to give up everything for *me.* That was scary."

"But you wouldn't let me do that , either."

"I want you to be happy."

"So naturally that means refusing to marry me." His crooked smile told her he was teasing. Sort of.

"If that's what it takes."

"I want to kiss you."

"And I want to kiss you, but Rance and Lani just brought the tack in." She gestured to the reddish horse with a white patch on his forehead who was poking his nose over the stall door. "Sweetie-Pie, I'd like you to meet Kieran Haggerty. He's from Ireland, but someday soon you'll be seeing a lot of him."

She said all that without a catch in her voice. She was proud of that.

_35_

"You're a natural, buddy."

"Thanks. Don't feel like one." Kieran glanced over at Rance standing next to Sara. Lani had gone into the house, but Rance had stayed to see how the greenhorn managed the first ride of his life.

Or maybe his goal was a conversation with Sara. Kieran couldn't hear what it was about since he only caught pieces of it when Pie wandered over that way. He could guess, though.

Rance wanted Sara to move to the ranch almost as much as he did. The fella clearly hoped this relationship would have a happy ending. He might be luring Sara with the prospect of trading in her car for a truck like his. Or the joy of having a horse of her own.

Maybe he'd tried that approach with Lani and that's how they'd ended up arseways with each other. Bribery wasn't in Kieran's nature. He didn't plan to lay out reasons she should sacrifice her chosen path for him. Bad enough his granny had made that sacrifice.

He needed to hear that story. She could've started teaching once his mum was in school. That would have given her sixteen or seventeen years in the classroom. Why hadn't she gone back once he was in school? Grief. That was his best guess.

"Kieran!" Sara called over to him. "He's heading for the flowers by the porch! Don't let him eat them!"

He brought his focus back to the horse under him. Pie was going straight for a bed of flowers. He pulled back on the reins and called out *whoa*. Pie stopped. Now what?

"Turn him around!"

"Got it!" What had Sara told him about changing direction? Feck it all, he couldn't remember. "D'ya know voice commands, then, Pie?"

Turning his head, the horse gazed at him.

"Ya look like ya do and *whoa* worked." He swept his hand out. "*Right*." He pointed again. "*Right,* lad."

Pie shook his head and stayed where he was.

"Ya don't fancy that direction? Fair enough. *Left*." He swept out his other arm. "*Left,* laddie. That way."

Rance's laughter told him he might be making an eejit of himself. He swiveled in the saddle and here came that fella, striding toward him, a grin on his puss.

"I see the problem, buddy."

"I'm an eejit who can't ride?"

"Nope. This routine is boring. It's not holding your attention. Take your left foot out of the stirrup. I'm coming up."

"Where?" But he did as he was told. "I take up the whole saddle, mate."

"But not the whole horse." Shoving his boot in the stirrup, Rance swung up behind him. "You can put your foot back in."

"Where are you putting yours?"

"Don't need to put them anywhere."

"You won't fall off?"

"Not with this horse." He put his arms around Keiran's waist. "Give me the reins."

He handed them over and like magic Pie turned around and pointed toward the ranch road. "How'd you do that?"

"Neck reining. Pie, um, doesn't respond to hand signals." His voice sounded funny.

"I learned that, yeah." He looked for Sara. She had her mobile out pointed at him.

"Grab hold of the horn and grip with your legs. We're going for a ride."

Kieran barely had time to do that before Pie took off. His arse left the saddle, smacked down and lifted again. "Feck, mate! Ya out ta b-banjax my s-sex life?"

"Use your thigh muscles and engage your core."

Ignoring that advice, he stood in the stirrups so his arse didn't make contact at all. It was a wonder his hat was still on. "Are we g-galloping?"

"Trotting."

"That's it? Feels f-faster."

"It's a fast trot. Tricky to learn."

"I b-believe ya."

"Next one's more fun. Cantering."

"Then g-galloping?"

"Not today. Cantering's enough. There's a rhythm to it. It's like sex. Match the horse's rhythm and you're golden."

"How d'ya switch g-gears?"

"I squeeze with my legs and nudge his side with my heels. Ready?"

"If it's s-smoother than this, I'm m-more than r-ready."

"Then here we go."

In an instant, Pie transformed from a jackhammer to a rocking chair. Kieran slowly lowered his arse to the saddle with a happy sigh. He savored the breeze in his face and the scenery flashing by as his body moved with the fluid motions of the horse.

"Like it?"

"It's craic, this is. Couldn't ya just skip over the trot and go straight to the canter?"

"Not if you wanna be a cowboy. Cowboys do it all."

"I was afraid of that."

Rance laughed. "You'll learn fast, once you're here for good and can practice. Any idea how soon that'll be?"

"Before snow comes, that's for sure."

"You and Granny will be here for Christmas?"

"We will."

"Awesome."

He hadn't put that together. Sara would be here for Christmas, too. She'd already said as much. Something to look forward to, even if it was only a few days. "If you don't mind me asking, what were you and Sara—"

"We were talking about you."

"Were you, now?"

"Just kidding. I was tossing out possibilities, hoping to get her thinking outside the box. I'm all for the principle that her folks taught her and Lani, but I don't believe in straitjackets, either."

"Did she fancy any of the things you mentioned?"

"We'll see." He drew back on the reins and guided Pie in a half circle. "Time to wrap this up. Clint'll be here soon."

"If you're in a hurry, we'd better stick with the canter."

He chuckled. "Sorry, buddy. Pie needs to cool down. We'll be trotting back."

<u>36</u>

Sara had no doubt that Kieran belonged at Rowdy Ranch, and his hysterical first experience on Pie gave her a great sneak preview of what awaited him as he became part of the McLintock clan. That episode was only the beginning of what would be a lifelong adventure.

Soon after the tolerant Sweetie-Pie was turned out to join the herd in the pasture, Clint arrived to give Rance a ride to the Buffalo.

Kieran grabbed the opportunity to give Clint the news, which he received with enthusiasm. He gave a cheerful tap to the horn as they pulled away.

"He's really happy you'll be joining the family." Sara turned and started back toward the house.

Kieran fell into step beside her. "Seems he is, yeah."

"Looks like Angie's back from taking my folks to the cabin site. They must have driven in while we were hanging out watching the horses in the pasture." She checked her phone. "And it's lunchtime already."

"And here I was hoping we'd have a wee moment alone."

She met his gaze. The fire in his blue eyes took her breath away. Inside the house everyone was gathering for lunch and all she wanted was to run away with Kieran.

"I miss you." Already his accent was shifting back, no longer a perfect echo of his granny's.

"I miss you, too. But today's all about your exciting announcement. Angie and my folks will want to hear it."

"And I want to share it. I just...."

"I know."

He paused before going up the porch steps. "Rance asked how soon we'll be coming over. I said we'd be here for Christmas."

"You will?" She'd see him then. What a lovely surprise. "You can make it happen that fast?"

"Granny may be getting on in years, but when she's on a mission, she's up to ninety."

"Go, Granny!"

"I'll not be holding her back. The idea of seeing you at Christmas... it's grand to think of, yeah?"

"Yeah."

"We won't be sneaking over to Rance's cabin."

"Well, probably not, but... the logistics will be...."

"Leave it to me, lass. Just know that we'll be sharing a bed and it won't be a secret anymore."

"Fine with me." She'd go along with anything, but how in the world could he create a temporary love nest?

She couldn't picture it. Or much of anything beyond this week. She used to be able to look ahead and anticipate at least the next few months on the calendar. Now it was a jigsaw puzzle with huge sections missing.

A while ago Rance had tossed in a few random pieces from a completely different puzzle and she couldn't make those fit either. But there was one piece, an idea that had come to her when she'd ridden back from town with Kieran.

In the rush of recent events, she'd lost it. That idea might be critical, but she wouldn't know unless she remembered what it was.

"Sara?"

"What?"

"You were staring off into space, like you had a vision."

"I didn't, but I could use one. Listen, when we go in, I'd like to peel off and slip into the library for a little while."

"With me?" His eyes lit up.

"No, sorry." She touched his cheek to soften the rejection. "I need time alone. I have some thinking to do. If anybody asks, just say...."

"The truth, yeah? That you need time alone?"

"Sure. That works."

Dipping his head, he brushed his lips over hers. "To hold me until tonight."

She almost grabbed him.

He smiled. "Makes my heart sing when you look at me like that."

And now she was a puddle of goo. If he swept her up and carried her off to his car, she wouldn't stop him.

Instead he gestured toward the steps and she marched up to the porch because it was the right thing to do.

Sam greeted them at the door and followed Kieran when he patted his thigh and made for the living room and the sound of animated conversation.

Ducking into the library, Sara quietly closed the door. The peaceful environment drew a sigh of relief from her tight chest. She'd been on emotional overload ever since Kieran had walked into Hannigan's.

She cherished every moment of being with him. But after non-stop drama, she needed to catch her breath, order her thoughts, figure out where the hell she was headed and whether a course correction was called for.

She browsed the shelves, finding many old favorites from classics to current popular writers, from Jane Austin to Nora Roberts, Edgar Allen Poe to Stephen King. *Stephen King.* That was it! The missing piece!

Excitement shot through her as she pulled out her phone and searched for Stephen King tours. Adventuring Travel came up, but so did several boutique operations. She zeroed in on one that advertised intimate tours limited to six people.

A pleasant sounding woman named Sybil answered and launched into a long list of the services they offered, from the lowest tier to the highest. Sybil suggested that a meet and greet with King himself might be arranged under certain circumstances. No guarantee of course.

Sara took notes on her phone and was about to thank her and hang up, but Sybil was clearly having a slow day. She kept talking. Sara didn't mind. This was exactly the type of information she was looking for.

Sybil told her they were creating similar tours all over the country involving well-known authors, both living and dead. Features would include visiting the author's hometown, exploring various book locations and touring the author's residence if they or their heirs were amenable.

"You need to check back in a month or so," she said. "We recently learned M.R. Morrison's secret identity and we're determined to have a presence in Wagon Train, Montana."

Sara almost dropped her phone. "Oh, really?"

"Our preliminary research tells us there's a bit of local flavor and the town's name is great, but otherwise Wagon Train needs to step it up. Their western wear store is called Hannigan's, if you can believe it. Sounds like an Irish pub, not a place where you buy boots and cowboy hats."

"Maybe so, but I doubt the owners would—"

"They will if they want to be featured on the tour. Oh, and it gets worse. A little bookshop in town features M.R. Morrison, but they call it L'Amour and More. Hel-*lo.* Call it *Morrison's*, right? These people need help with a capital H."

"Interesting."

"We wouldn't lead with those suggestions, of course. We just need to get our foot in the door and then gradually bring the town up to speed. We can assume that the author, who's a woman it turns out, will be looking for someone to manage the tourist angle now that she's come out of hiding. And we'll be there to offer our services."

"I see."

"We've run into some trouble getting in touch with her, but we'll break through that slight roadblock soon. We're persistent."

"I can tell. And thank you so much. This has been very informative."

"Would you like to book a Stephen King tour?"

"Let me check on my friend's schedule. Thanks for all your help. Have a great day." She disconnected.

Was Desiree in her office? It was on the other side of the revolving bookcase, but the unspoken household rule was that only an emergency justified disturbing her.

Smiling at her ridiculous self, she moved back, opened her arms and used her deepest voice. "*Open sesame.*"

Laughter came from the other side and the bookcase revolved. Desiree stood there grinning. "The kids used to do that *all* the time. I haven't heard it in years."

"Did I disturb you?"

"Not really. I heard you on the phone and I wondered who you were talking to. Or not talking to. Whoever was on the other end must have been a chatterbox."

"They were. I'll give you the name of the company and if you ever hear from them, show them the door. They're terrible."

"Oh? What do they do?"

"They create tours revolving around well-known authors — the settings for their books, their hometown, maybe even a tour of their house and exclusive meet and greets. You don't want to have anything to do with them."

"Not if you don't like them. Out of curiosity, why'd you call them?"

"Just an idea I had." And it was still half-baked. Was she crazy to suggest it before she'd worked out the details?

"I wonder if we're on the same page. Lucky, Oksana, Trent and I have been talking about doing something similar. The tourists will come, and if we don't organize things for them to do, they may get up to mischief, like trying to find Rowdy Ranch."

"You mentioned something to me about that. You said you were worried about loss of privacy."

"So you decided to research tour companies for us? That's so kind of you. If you're willing to keep looking, I'll pay you for your time. After all, this is your area."

"Actually, I called to gather ideas. I was so horrified by what that woman said that my first thought was *oh, my God, what if Desiree accidentally hires someone like that?*"

"What was your second thought?"

"Now that I'm talking to you I feel a little presumptuous saying this, but my second thought was *I should do it.*"

Her eyes brightened. "It was?"

"Please understand that I'd need time to come up with a workable plan, but after listening to Sybil, I got excited about generating similar ideas for—"

"Would this be a side gig? In addition to your regular job?"

"No. It's too big, too important to be a side gig. If it's done right, it'll be a fulltime job."

"Oh, Sara." Desiree looked ready to explode. "Are you saying what I think you're saying? That you'd quit your job and do this instead?"

"Yes, but maybe you don't envision having someone handle it fulltime. Your budget might not—"

"Are you kidding? This is a dream come true! We've wanted you from the beginning, but you've been so enthusiastic about staying in your current job that it seemed pointless to ask."

"You talked about hiring me?"

"Weeks ago, but after all you've said about loving Trenton and your job, the idea had to come from you. The most I allowed myself was mentioning we need to deal with the tourist situation. You didn't pick up on it. You were still focused on moving up in your company and finally getting to Ireland."

"Ireland." Sara laughed. "I was fixated on that, but instead, Ireland came to me."

"I suppose it did. He did."

"And now I still want to see Ireland, but I want Kieran as my tour guide. We can plan to go sometime in the future."

"Are you sure about all this?" Desiree looked her in the eye. "Because I'd hate for you to wake up tomorrow and realize you'd been hijacked by the emotions swirling around today."

"It's been a lot. By the way, Granny was willing to move to New Jersey so I could keep my job and marry Kieran."

"Wow."

"After she hung up, we discussed both scenarios and I couldn't see Granny thriving there. She will thrive here, though."

"Please tell me you didn't decide to take on this project to please his granny."

"I didn't. But I won't lie. The prospect of living in the same zip code as Kieran is a major draw."

"You'd be giving up your job to be with him. I thought that violated your principles."

"I'm giving up the job but not the career. This morning Rance was talking about self-employment as an option and I couldn't see it."

"That boy! I'll bet Lucky told him we wanted you but it had to be your idea. He was hoping to steer you toward it."

"To be fair, he didn't come out and suggest this idea."

"If he had I would have blistered his ears."

"He didn't. I had to work it out on my own. It's a fabulous challenge for a travel planner — orchestrating tours that please your readers and protect your privacy at the same time. I can't wait to brainstorm with you guys."

"I can tell you're excited. I can see it in your face. But let's do this, just to make sure it isn't adrenaline talking. Give it twenty-four hours."

She shook her head. "It's not just adrenaline. This is it. Lani's the only person who won't like it, but she'll be happy for me in the end. I don't need twenty-four hours."

"Then take the time for me, so I won't worry that you'll wake up tomorrow with a change of heart."

"I won't."

"Please. Let's keep this between us at least until tomorrow morning. If you're still excited about this prospect, we'll go with it."

She dragged in a breath. "Okay. I'll bow to your wisdom. It's probably a good idea."

"I promise you it is. Let the concept settle in your mind and in your body. A week would be better, but we don't have a week."

"I couldn't stand to wait that long, but I can handle one day. I assume you'll tell Andy, though."

"I will, but only him. And obviously you can tell Kieran, but... I advise you not to. Not until you're sure. This means too much. You don't want to tell him and then change your mind."

"Sure don't." But not telling him would be extremely difficult, especially if they ended up alone today. She'd make sure that didn't happen until tonight. Then all bets were off.

37

"She hates me." Kieran sent a ball sailing toward a pocket, then another one. He was getting the hang of this game, but then he'd used these two hours to practice while he waited for Rance to come home from the Buffalo.

"I guaran-damn-tee she doesn't." Rance only had a few minutes before he had to leave to get Sara. No time to test Kieran's new skills.

"I know she doesn't hate me. I just said that because I'm frustrated. She wouldn't change her mind that fast. Right before lunch she looked at me like I was the pot of gold at the end of the rainbow."

"Which is how she feels. Sure, you guys have some hurdles, but she's crazy about you."

"Then why did she work so bleedin' hard this afternoon and evening making sure we were never alone? I couldn't even get her alone to ask her why she didn't want to be alone with me."

Rance snorted.

"It's not funny. I'm worried."

"Sorry, but you should hear yourself. You're sounding a little crazy."

"I am a little crazy. After that adoring look, she went into the library to think. Then she acted like I had germs. I'm worried she came to some realization about me that I don't want to hear."

"Did she cancel tonight's event?"

"No."

"Then realization or no realization, she still craves your body. You can work with that."

"Meaning what?"

"When she gets here, whatever you do, don't ask her what's wrong."

"But I need ta know!"

"Do you really? Chances are it'll freak you out or start a fight."

"Thanks for putting that in my head."

"Stay with me, here. You have a strong sexual connection, so you're gonna lean into it. Make love to her like there's no tomorrow and pray you'll make her so happy she'll forget whatever burr was under her saddle."

He chuckled. "Burr under her saddle. I fancy that."

"By all means take it. Work it into conversations. It's a cowboyism."

"A whatzit?"

"Anything that makes you think of cowboys. I made it up, but turns out it's a word."

"Cowboyism. I fancy that one, too." He hit a combo and sent two balls into two different pockets. "I appreciate the advice, mate, but I'm gonna ask her what's wrong."

"Don't do it, buddy. You'll regret it. In fact, here's your game plan. She pulls up — I'm sure she'll be driving — and you go straight to the truck, help her out and hustle her in. If she tries to talk, kiss her."

"I can't kiss and hustle all at once. I'd make a mess of it."

"I'll bet you can. It's all in staying focused. Get naked ASAP and go to work. If you can't keep her too busy to talk, you're not the man I think you are. And I'm outta here." Grabbing his keys, he left.

Kieran snapped the pool cue into its holder and tucked the balls in the pockets. Then he used the dimmer switch on the light over the pool table. The bedroom was ready—clean sheets turned back, condom on the bedside table, table lamps on low.

Should he consider Rance's approach? No. He wanted to find out why Sara had acted that way. Sure, she didn't want to broadcast their relationship, but she'd taken things to extremes. She hadn't done that the night before.

Then again, he could always ask her after the fact. She'd expect him to be eager. They'd missed out last night. If Rance had the right of it, then questioning her before they made love might banjax the whole program.

Last time she'd arrived without underwear, which would fit nicely into Rance's scenario. He'd be the plonker who'd slow things down since he was fully dressed.

Unless he wasn't. But jeans on his bare arse would not be a pleasant experience. He'd brought sweatpants, though. Hadn't worn 'em yet.

Dashing into the bedroom, he found them in the bottom of his duffle and began ripping off his clothes. How long had it been since Rance drove off? He couldn't be caught in the middle of undressing.

Or naked, which he was when the rumble of Midnight Thunder sounded in the distance. He yanked on the sweatpants. Boots? Nope. He'd go barefoot rather than look like an eejit in boots and sweatpants.

Wasn't going out there bare-chested, either. That would be a wee bit too obvious.

Grabbing a T-shirt, he pulled it on as he ran towards the door and jerked it open. Sara was just driving in. Made it.

She flashed the lights. What did that mean? No matter, he was going for it. Jogging down the steps gave him a hint of what naked volleyball would be like. Not a fan. The soles of his feet weren't happy with the gravel parking area, either.

Stay focused. He opened the driver's side door and reached for... Rance?

"Other side, buddy. Other side."

"You said for sure—"

"She didn't want to. I flashed my lights."

"How was I to know what that meant?"

"It means something's *different.* You're supposed to stop what you're doing and do something else." Then he started laughing. "Nice shirt. Make sure she reads it."

"Feck." He'd snatched up the one that said *Irishmen do it better... and longer.* Granny had told him to take it and find himself a wife. He'd thought she was kidding but he'd packed it just to make her laugh.

"Hey, guys." Sara came around from the other side. "Is this a private conversation or can I — whoa, Kieran. I pegged you as the modest, unassuming type, but—"

"Clearly he's the bold and daring type."

"That's me, alright." She'd worn the same outfit as the first night. Hallelujah. "See ya later, mate." Walking toward Sara, he cupped his hands under her sweet arse and lifted her off her feet.

She clutched his shoulders for support. "I see we're not waiting for Rance to—"

"Not waiting for anything." He claimed her mouth and started for the porch. Kissing while climbing steps wasn't as bouncy as riding a fast trot, but he had to concentrate to make sure he didn't bite her.

As they crossed the porch, she broke away, panting. "I have something to—"

"I need you." He leaned in and kissed her like he meant it. And he absolutely did. She had him in a very tight grip, squeezing his cock against her open thighs. They were separated by two layers of flimsy material and her leggings were already damp.

He nudged the door closed with his foot without losing that all-important kiss. Next he slid his arm under her arse to free up one hand. Her boots had to go. It wasn't an easy task, but he managed it, leaving both boots in the living room.

The goal was at hand. Another two minutes, three, tops, and he'd be rocking her world and his. Walking faster added movement to that critical area that was not just damp. Soaked, it was.

She moaned softly and lifted her mouth away. "Before we do this, I have—"

"Nay, lass." *Nay*? Who was he, a time traveling knight in shining armor? Yes, by God. He was her knight in shining armor. "Whisht, now. Let me love ya."

Stepping into the bedroom, he managed to keep his mouth on hers as he laid her out on the bed and worked her out of her leggings. Then he had an inspiration.

And a hunger. Climbing onto the bed, he moved over her and interrupted their kiss long enough to pull her shirt off. Then he went back to kissing her... everywhere.

She tried to say something as he nuzzled her breasts, so he scooted up and recaptured her mouth, keeping those tempting lips busy while he caressed every inch he could reach.

His fingertips tingled from the pleasure of touching her soft skin. He roamed at will, finally sliding his hand between her thighs. Ah, he had her, now. Lifting his head, he gulped for air.

She was breathing fast, too. "Kieran... there's something I—"

She gasped as he thrust his fingers deep. Holding her gaze, he stroked her slowly, then faster, savoring the approach of her climax, treating himself to a view of the fireworks in her eyes.

She came, her skin flushing a beautiful pink and her cries filling his heart with joy. Sliding down between her thighs, he took her up again and her cries were even wilder the second time.

Slipping away from the bed, he whipped off his shirt and sweatpants, put on the condom and was back, gliding his cock into the warmth of her welcoming body.

A glow in her green eyes, she wrapped him in her arms and moved with him as he coaxed them both toward a glorious release. She came again, and he joined her.

Whatever had happened today was nothing compared to this. They'd found the most precious gift of all.

As his breathing slowed, he gazed at her, the girl of his dreams. "I love you."

"I love you, too. Will you marry me?"

He gulped. "What?"

"Will. You. Marry. Me."

"But I thought—"

"Go take care of the condom. I have something to tell you."

38

Longest day ever. But the ending was turning out to be spectacular. Sara lay sprawled out on the bed, smiling. Desiree had wanted to give her time to think, and she had used that time well. Kieran would have been a terrible distraction so she'd stayed far away from that tempting Irishman.

She'd confused him in the process, and for that she was sorry. But the perspective she'd gained to consider all the ramifications of her decision had been so valuable.

She'd pictured leaving her job and saying goodbye to her wonderful bosses and co-workers. She'd stay for the required two weeks, of course, which would give her a chance to let everyone know how much she appreciated their friendship and mentoring.

But in the end, she had to agree with Rance. Creating her own business and being her own boss was vastly more appealing.

Leaving her personal friends would be tough. But many of her oldest ones had moved away and she'd invite all her buddies to visit her in Montana. As for leaving her hometown, whenever she missed the familiar sights and sounds, she'd come back for a few days with Kieran and show him where she grew up.

Leaving her sister, especially when she'd be without any family there, was the hardest part. But Lani wasn't tied to her office like Sara had been. Their parents had air miles going to waste so Lani could make frequent trips to Rowdy Ranch and work remotely.

Kieran walked out of the bathroom gloriously naked. "I'm confused."

She sat up and tucked a pillow behind her back. "That's because you wouldn't let me talk when I first got here."

"That was Rance's idea." He grabbed a pillow and copied her setup.

"Huh?"

"I was going to ask you why you avoided me after your time in the library, but Rance said I was better off making mad love to you instead, so you'd forget about the burr under your saddle."

She grinned. "Well, guess what? I haven't forgotten."

He sighed. "Grand."

"Don't worry. You'll love this burr." She laid out her plans, which were far more detailed than they'd been during her short discussion with Desiree. She'd been making notes on her phone all day.

Kieran quit leaning against the pillow. He shifted around to face her, his gaze locked with hers.

"So that's it." She'd unconsciously mirrored his position. "What do you think?"

"One question. Are you doing all this for me?"

"No."

"You'd do it even if I stayed in Ireland, then?"

She rolled that around in her mind. "I would. I've fallen in love with this idea. I've also fallen in love with Rowdy Ranch."

"I'm just the whipped topping, then?"

"I wouldn't say that." She cupped his face in both hands. "You shaved for me."

"Yes, ma'am." His blue eyes glittered. "I'd do anything for you, even live in New Jersey. But I won't stand by silent as a fencepost if you're throwing away a job you love because I showed up in your life."

"Listen to me. I know you have good hearing. Desiree asked me to take time to make sure this is the right move. That's what I was doing today. I avoided you and concentrated on what I was giving up, not what I was getting. This decision is absolutely the right one."

"And you didn't gloss over anything?"

"I did not. This is my future, here with the McLintocks, my family, Granny, and you. So I'll ask again. Will you marry me?"

The intensity in his gaze morphed into something deeper. Clasping her hands, he glanced down and carefully slid his fingers through hers. He swallowed. When he looked up, his eyes were moist. "It would be my honor, lass."

Her throat tightened. "I love you," she whispered.

"I love you. I always have. And I always will." Leaning forward, he touched his lips to hers.

The light press of his mouth was tender, almost reverent. Tears slipped down her cheeks. All they'd needed was a miracle. Thanks to some very special people, they'd created one.

* * * * *

Rance's story is coming your way just in time for the holidays. Watch for
SAVING THE COWBOY'S CHRISTMAS
this November!

* * * * *

New York Times bestselling author Vicki Lewis Thompson's love affair with cowboys started with the Lone Ranger, continued through Maverick, and took a turn south of the border with Zorro. She views cowboys as the Western version of knights in shining armor, rugged men who value honor, honesty and hard work. Fortunately for her, she lives in the Arizona desert, where broad-shouldered, lean-hipped cowboys abound. Blessed with such an abundance of inspiration, she only hopes that she can do them justice.

For more information about this prolific author, visit her website and sign up for her newsletter. She loves connecting with readers.

VickiLewisThompson.com